CW00644749

CRAZY *FOOLISH* ROBOTS

BOOK 1: The Robot Galaxy Series

Adeena Mignogna

CRAZY FOOLISH ROBOTS

Copyright © 2021 by Adeena Mignogna

All rights reserved. No part of this publication may be reproduced or used in any manner without written permission of the copyright owner except for the use of quotations in a book review.

This is a work of fiction. Names, characters, places, and incidents are the product of the author's imagination. Any resemblance to actual persons, living or dead, events, or locales, or actual robots, functioning or not, is entirely coincidental.

ISBN: 979-8-9855963-3-5

Edited by: Carolani Bartell

Book cover design by: Ebooklaunch.com

Published by Crazy Robot, LLC

The Robot Galaxy Series

ACKNOWLEDGMENTS

I would like to thank first and foremost my hubby and kiddos for all the time I ignored them to work on this book. I also want to thank them for listening to me go on and on about Ruby and the robots and all the problems I encountered writing this.

Next, I need to thank all my beta readers who read some or all of the manuscript in various forms and provided incredibly helpful feedback: Dora, Anna, Clay, Duff, Lisa, Diana, Sara, Ryan, David and David (no relation), and Clay.

Third, I want to thank my copy editor, Carolani, who completely grokked the voice of the book and makes me wonder why I ever hesitated with the decision to hire a copy editor.

Lastly, I have to once again thank my family because they're going to be the ones who have to put up with me as I finish the next book in the series…

Crazy Foolish Robots

Before We Begin

Out of the millions of email messages traveling daily between Earth and Astroll 2, rarely did any have the power over nineteen-year-old Ruby's life the way this one did. Yet, the email was not addressed to her, nor did she see it, nor did she have any idea it had ruined her plans.

How did this happen?

Quite simply, the email was addressed to a mister Robt Plampton, station director of Astroll 2. Located in the heart of the asteroid belt, Astroll 2 was Ruby's home from the age of seven. The email stated that the staff was to prepare for an upcoming installation of a series of AI applications that were meant to greatly benefit Astroll 2 and the corporation which owned it. That, in itself, should have been quite harmless; and it should have improved the quality of Ruby's life, as someone who lived on said station that would be receiving the enhanced AI.

However, Ruby, counting every day until she turned twenty-one, was still under the guardianship and sponsorship of her two uncles, Blake and Logan. They weren't blood relatives but her mother's best friends. Ruby's mother had no other family to speak of when she perished, so she left her young daughter in their care.

Ruby's only living blood relative was her grandmother, who had been in an assisted living facility prior to Ruby's conception. Her medical transcript cited various permanent psychoses which prevented her from living on her own. Such as her tendency to routinely knock on the neighbor's door in the middle of the night, half-dressed, asking if the aliens had finally responded to her email.

The final relevant detail affecting Ruby's life was the fact that her

Uncle Logan was an odorist. His primary responsibility was to ensure that the smells of items and materials brought to Astroll 2 were not offensive. Primarily, the toxicity of any given material was mechanically inspected and then listed on the paperwork of said items. But in order to determine how pleasant or offensive a smell might be, especially in the small, confined rooms of a space station with continually recycled air, a sensitive and willing human nose was required.

Until now. Now, an AI could do this job. Which meant that Ruby and her family, now obsolete to the station, would be returning to Earth.

Emails were not the only items on their way to Astroll 2. Several ships were noted to be in various phases of their journey from Earth and Mars. All these ships existed in station records as expected, incoming arrivals.

Yet, one particular ship was not on the arrival manifest at all. It was one unknown to humankind, and it was on approach from outside the human-known solar system. No human occupied this ship, either. Only a solitary, intelligent robot.

Neither Ruby nor the robot could imagine that their trajectories would soon be intersecting, intertwining their lives in unimaginable ways.

Chapter 1

> Ruby <

"How many days until my 21st birthday?" Ruby spoke into her communicuff.

She darn well knew the answer, so it was the perfect way to test her communicuff. It was exactly 429 days.

That was the day when she no longer needed the sponsorship of her uncles to stay on Astroll 2. That was also the day she could legally join the Titan expedition. Ruby knew that a long time ago, eighteen was the age of full emancipation. After the Grey Matter Coup of 2113, the world government agreed that a mature prefrontal cortex was a defining characteristic of adulthood. While this level of neural development rarely happened prior to twenty-five, twenty-one years old was selected. With the exception that an individual could prove maturity via a set of brain scans. Ruby was fortunate that Astroll 2 had a brain-scanning facility. But as of her last scan a month and a half ago, she wasn't even close. Despite all the brain training games, extra omega-3s added to everything she ate and drank, and even ordering a special device to wear while sleeping that was supposed to help, her brain was determined to take its time reaching maturity. She *felt* old enough, but science disagreed. She would have to wait out the 429 days until her twenty-first birthday.

So, when a disembodied voice replied, "three thousand seven hundred point two," Ruby let out a heavy sigh. Her communicuff was malfunctioning. That's why she had been waiting at the Care Center entrance for the last half hour. She arrived early to ensure she was first in line. Perhaps *too* early.

Ruby looked up from her cuff-wrapped arm and shifted her eyes to the closed window in front of her. Unfortunately, she couldn't trust the cuff to give the correct time either, so she wasn't sure exactly how much longer she had to wait. Maybe 30 seconds. Maybe seventeen minutes. She inwardly cursed herself for even having to rely on technology and not an internal clock for time, but was told that was normal for humans who lived for years inside a space station.

A sign was visible in the window, but the black lettering had worn away with time. The words 'Care Center' were in a large and crisp Sans Serif font. Underneath, in a font made to resemble handwriting, were the words "If we don't take care of you" and then nothing but scratched metal. Care didn't extend to caring for the sign, apparently.

Ruby blinked at the sad, gray sign and couldn't help but empathize with it. For she too knew what it was like to feel like time was wearing her down. Recently, her days had been blurring together. On a typical day, her uncles and cousin were out of the shared living space before she woke up. That was her own fault for sleeping in. Once, family breakfast time was something she wouldn't miss, but she couldn't drag herself out of bed lately. As she got up later and later, her breakfasts came to consist of an empty table, boring news briefs, and a cold meal she couldn't be bothered to re-heat. The only remnants of her family's morning resided in whatever note her uncles left her that particular day. Usually, a reminder to do the bone and muscle-maintaining exercise she was supposed to do, but always 'forgetting.' After, she would go off to work.

As she looked ahead to another 429 days of sameness, she still felt like it beat the unpleasant hell on Earth. It had been over a decade since she lived on Earth, but between what she remembered and what she read about on the news feeds, to Ruby, it was a place overrun by all manner of robots and AIs.

Earth had become automated to a point where more robots were employed than human beings. Robots manufactured goods and moved them between different facilities. They prepared food. They were security guards. They cleaned floors. Robots (with all levels of AI) replaced innumerable jobs, including the one that irked Ruby the most: the pilots.

Out here, Ruby was a pilot. And anyone could tell you that she was a good one. Out here, Ruby believed that it was still too unpredictable and dangerous to let robots pilot around the asteroids. Humans were still needed, Ruby included.

On this mundane Tuesday—now a week after Robt Plampton opened and read the aforementioned email—this outwardly minor issue with her communicuff forced Ruby out of her routine. And at the worst time, too. Today, she had plans to meet with one of the Titan expedition's leading scientists. Not a great day to require tech support, especially when the support available would subject her to such a nonsensical process.

The Care Center window slid open, revealing a FUFE (fresh up from Earth) who Ruby recognized from one of the recent loads of new station workers.

"Can I help you?" he said. His voice was taut and toneless.

"My communicuff has gone a little haywire," Ruby replied, holding up her cuff, which filled two-thirds of her arm. "It's not responding to my commands. At least, not correctly."

"Did you try resetting it?"

Ruby tried awfully hard to do something with her eyes other than roll them at the suggestion.

"Yes, twice."

After a useless half an hour, the Care Center FUFE proved to be no help, and Ruby was instructed to call Earth's Care Center Service Heart. Ruby exhaled a sigh of defeat. Calling them was only ever a last resort. No matter how simple or complicated the issue, a call with the Heart guaranteed to eat up at least half a morning. The Care Givers on the other end were to walk the unfortunate caller through a script that laid out a series of rudimentary symptoms and solutions. They were duplicates of what the local Care Center worked through, but with the added time delay of a conversation back to Earth, in addition to the fact that deviations from the script were entirely unacceptable.

Astroll 2 could best be described as a long rotating cylinder with a ring wrapped around its mid-section. Ruby made her way from the Care Center, located in the outermost portion of the station's central ring inwards, one level to where most living quarters were located, including hers. That's where Ruby found herself for the second half of this particular Tuesday morning, exactly one week after her life's future path was unknowingly altered.

At least in her quarters she could keep an eye on a reliable clock built into the wall. She would not allow herself to be late for her meeting with Dr. Guerrero.

An hour later, Ruby was on a video call with the image of what could have been a clone of the FUFE at the local Care Center.

"When did it last work?" the image said. Ruby knew it hadn't been working since at least the previous afternoon. She had been approaching the promenade and happened to overhear a conversation two older women were having. They were discussing the new AI that was going to be installed in the station.

Actually, 'happened to' was not entirely correct. Ruby did make a habit of eavesdropping on other's conversations when they were within earshot. She had no qualms about listening in. They were, after all, in a public space. If she wasn't meant to hear, they should have stayed in private.

Thinking she might've missed something in the news—as she generally did, since news wasn't her thing—she raised her arm and attempted to access information on this alleged new AI. The display hovered over the communicuff, but it wasn't the news. It was the day's menu at the mess. She swiped that away and attempted to bring up her email.

But the device decided to call Uncle Logan, and she couldn't hang it up in time to stop it from going through. The face of a familiar, smiling, handsome man materialized on the screen.

"Ruby! Sweetie! Are you going to join us in the mess for dinner? Uncle Blake and I promised Sebastian we'd eat by the windows." Uncle Logan's bright eyes were always full of love and hope and endless patience for Ruby.

Despite her own frustrations, Ruby couldn't help but smile back. "Yes, Uncle Logan. I'll meet you there."

"K, kiddo," Uncle Logan winked before he ended the call. Ruby caught a glance of Uncle Blake and Sebastian behind him.

Ruby attempted once more to get the device to do what she wanted. When she tried to bring up the day's menu at the mess, she succeeded in loading her email instead.

"Piece of junk," she said to herself, flicking away the holo-image.

Trying to explain any of this now to the Earth-bound Care Giver was futile. It didn't help that the problem wasn't reproducible in any predictable way. It *really* didn't help that Ruby was on a bit of a time crunch.

But she remained in the living area of her tiny quarters, tossing a bean bag up and catching it to ease her impatience. It did not have the satisfying punch of the catch of a bean bag in standard Earth gravity, but that was a feature of Astroll 2 life that Ruby had adjusted to over the years.

"I'm going to walk you through a sequence of steps," said a voice emanating from the comm panel.

"Sure," said Ruby with her jaw clenched. She knew that was coming next and wished there was something she could say that would enable them to skip some steps.

"Take off the cuff and turn it over."

Pause. Ruby already had the cuff off.

"Press the soft reset buttons simultaneously."

Another pause. Ruby had already done this step as well. Her cuff was splayed out on the table as Ruby waited for the technician to get to step *eight*. One through seven were a standard set of steps, and she had performed them at the start of the call.

At step six, the technician paused. "Um, what version is your system?"

Ruby took a deep sigh, but appreciated that this tech was a little more up on his game than the local guy. "I'm still at 45BAI."

"You know an upgrade to version 51AI is available?"

"Yeah, I don't want it," Ruby replied. Ruby had heard about the highly anticipated 51AI, which was indeed an AI. When she did a little research on 51AI, it seemed to be locked up tighter than Ultra Fort Knox, as the expression went. She was content with the non-AI version, the one she could hack and customize. As silly as it sounded to everyone around her, Ruby didn't want her cuff to think it was any smarter than she was.

"Are you sure?" the tech replied. "Most people love how it can anticipate your schedule and your needs and take action based on..."

None of this interested Ruby, so she cut him off. "Really, I'm good. Let's just keep going."

The tech then told Ruby they'd need to redo a few steps to account for the older version she had, now taking a tone with every step that implied she should upgrade. Finally, they made it back to step seven.

Eight was, "Let's try to access a current news report."

Ruby picked up the cuff and accessed the news.

Hovering over the cuff was the image of Juju, the genderless global pop-star, along with the text, "Juju just scheduled their first off-Earth concert in ten years ever since the accident..." Well, that was close in that it was current, but Ruby didn't consider it real news.

Ruby reported back her search results and then turned Juju off. Better to wait for tech support than rot her brain with celebrity gossip.

While waiting, Ruby took a brush through her dark hair, momentarily straightening out the curls, and pulled it back into a ponytail. Most people chose to buzz cut their hair in the low-gravity environments. Ruby couldn't stand the thought of looking like everyone else. She kept it a little past shoulder length and pulled it into a ponytail most of the time.

Ruby glanced at the time on the wall. The thought of being late for the meeting with Dr. Guerrero flashed in her mind. She thought about telling the Care Giver she was going to hang up, but skipped telling him and just hung up. She decided that she could live with a semi-malfunctioning cuff for now.

As she finished making sure she was visually presentable, the incomplete tech call and her non-functioning cuff continued to bother her. Images of face-palming memes and people pinching the upper bridge of their nose (symbols of frustration that were now as ubiquitous as a happy face or a heart) popped into Ruby's head without any particularly clever sayings. She had saved a few over the years that she enjoyed, but now, with her malfunctioning cuff, she couldn't locate them.

Would it be like this on Titan? She wondered. *No, not possible.*

They would be an independent operating entity, fending for themselves without any robots or advanced AI. Survival mode. Titan—the largest moon of Saturn and the furthest place in the solar system that humans had touched—was building a reputation as the new Earth. All the scientists and explorers involved in the expedition had the chance to make a significant impact on Titan's future as they planned to terraform it.

Three eccentric trillionaires formed the Zubrinics Titan Exploration Corporation, known as ZTEC. Their way of thinking almost directly reflected Ruby's, which is why she was anxious to go join them. A scientific base on an alien (sort-of) planet, with only the tech they needed to survive and function, all driven by human brains. Not AI. They would use machines to perform physical or fast calculations, of course. But thoughts, reasoning, and everything that made humans *human* would remain in the hands (or minds, rather) of the humans.

Ruby had seen specs of the communicuffs they used. They were simple devices to allow communication between people. They were timepieces. They stored calculation apps. Note taking apps. Apps to monitor the health of the user. All of which had been around for ages and used quite successfully before any Smart AI existed. Not a single Smart AI in the bunch.

Chapter 2

> Swell Driver <

Hurtling towards Earth at an unbelievable speed, someone else was also calculating the odds of its survival. That someone else was identified as Swell Driver 587 (by anything that needed to identify it, that is).

Swell Driver 587 was indeed a *swell* driver. Its primary function was piloting starships, and it performed that function very well. It did not perform other functions nearly as well, such as calculating statistics. So, when calculating the odds of its survival at 1 in 2583, this estimation might have been off by 75%. But the calculation of how off Swell Driver was also might have been off by roughly 53%.

Ordinarily, on a routine trip to pick up some artifacts and items of interest, calculating the odds of survival wouldn't need to happen mid-mission like this. Which is why there was no need for a Fantastic Calculator model to be aboard, although Swell Driver knew several back home. There wasn't even a Fine Calculator. This mission was considered low risk enough that it was only Swell Driver and the ship's computer. This setup satisfied Swell Driver.

But after passing within the vicinity of a Red Giant star which was in the middle of kicking off its outermost layers of matter and elements in a storm of radiation, the systems on Swell Drivers' ship became corrupted.

Much of the data necessary to navigate to this planet and back to Swell Driver's homeworld could have been affected. Luckily, Swell Driver determined that the vital navigation elements were intact. Actually, in the ship's computer, they had indeed become corrupted, but Swell Driver preserved these elements in its internal memory as a backup. It simply transferred the necessary data back into the ship's computer and continued on.

Swell Driver's next priority was to determine if the relevant data concerning the pickup cargo was intact. Recently, there had been several occurrences that hinted at a few issues with data corruption on a planetary scale. Like that time Swell Driver received duplicate instructions on a trip around its solar system that failed to include cargo. In the middle of the trip, Swell Driver figured out that a second part of the instruction set had to be missing.

What Swell Driver knew was that this current task involved obtaining biological organisms, known as 'Umans,' and transporting them back to its homeworld. Swell Driver checked the database on the ship's computer. The data records on the Umans looked complete, along with information on their sleeping patterns, eating habits, and top speed without the use of any external device. Swell Driver noted that picking up a small quantity of food was probably a good idea and pondered briefly on why steps to procure food was missing from its instructions.

Swell Driver's data included other helpful factoids as well. Such as how Umans consume leaves from many types of fruit trees and the legs of another native creature called 'rhinoceros.' Swell Driver was no expert on alien races, but thought it odd that these beings only ate the leaves while many other known biological races ate the fruit that came with these leaves. However, now wasn't a time to question the database. Questioning was what got one reprogrammed.

Unfortunately, the most essential piece of information was absent from the database: how to tell one biological lifeform from another on this particular planet. The data indicated that the amount of biological organisms that filled the Umans' homeworld was much higher than other known worlds. Swell Driver wasn't sure he could distinguish Umans from any of the other biological life there. The database contained various images and anatomical schematics, but none corresponded with labels—other than with the star system designation.

Swell Driver 587 spent the remainder of its trip sorting through the information on the ship's computer to see what it could keep versus delete. It had to make room for the massive amount of data it was going to be recording and sorting through once it arrived within the range of emissions coming from its destination planet.

Most of the species that researchers from Swell Driver's planet encountered were detected because of the various emissions they produced (as the species local to any planet learned to make use of the electromagnetic spectrum available to them). Swell Driver's ship came equipped with several large collecting devices to capture the most recent of these emissions.

Swell Driver's computer reported that this system was an electromagnetically noisy place, so it would receive data long before arrival. That was good, because from what little Swell Driver *did* know, it was going to need plenty of time to look at a great deal of data. Swell Driver wished a Great Data Organizer was assigned to this journey as well. Or at least a Fine Data Organizer. Yes, one of those would have done nicely.

Chapter 3

> Ruby <

Ruby checked the time once more before leaving her quarters. The evening before, she managed to arrange a meeting with Dr. Russell "Rush" Guerrero, one of the scientists from the Titan expedition. He was on his way back to Earth from Titan, stopping at Astroll 2 between. The ship from Titan arrived two weeks ago, and she had been trying to get in touch with him ever since.

He hadn't responded to any of her emails, probably because those were routed through an administrative filter back on Earth. But members of ZTEC didn't always stop at Astroll 2 on their way to and from Titan. This was Ruby's big chance to make an impression, establish a relationship, and hopefully convince one of the most important current team members that she was worth accepting. Maybe even making an exception to the minimum age rule.

So instead of relying on emails, knowing that he was headed back to Earth soon, she arranged to bump into him.

It was easy enough to do. Since there were no kitchenettes in temporary quarters, every visitor came through the mess hall at some point. She spent her day off hanging out there, waiting for Guerrero to come in and eat. She figured it was less desperate than sulking around his assigned temporary quarters.

He said he was happy to talk to a prospective team member.

And now here Ruby was, back in the mess hall. A full fifteen minutes before her appointment with Dr. Guerrero, and a mere few hours before his departure back to Earth.

Ruby grabbed a tray of food from the common carousel and found a table close enough to the door that Dr. Guerrero shouldn't have a problem spotting her, but not so close to others to invite attention. She wanted to give off a 'please don't talk to me right now' vibe without seeming overly rude. After all, she knew these people, had to see them most days, and would for another 429. Maybe less if this meeting was a success.

Most station residents who chose to eat in the mess sat close to the back wall, lined with windows, one of the few places on Astroll 2 that had windows at all. At least, this was common practice after becoming used to the spin of this ring of the station.

The view didn't offer much when the lights of the mess hall were on—you couldn't see the stars or Milky Way. The Sun was almost always in view, and the central window was also a smart screen that tracked and pointed to the location of all the planets. You could see ships coming and going from the station for as long as station lights were trained on them and while they were close enough for their own blinking lights to be visible to the human eye.

It became common practice for outgoing ships to code in morse code messages in their rear-facing blinking lights. Just to see who was paying attention and who got their jokes. More often than not, the outgoing message was a catchy final line from a movie or book. Ruby's favorite was the time that the ship *Heart of Gold* blinked, "So long and thanks for all the fish!" She began to laugh out loud but stopped when she realized that no one else was laughing along. One other person in the mess that day seemed to understand the message, but obviously not the joke when he said, "But we don't keep fish here."

Another quirk of the mess was stumbling into people that Ruby had no intention of chatting with. Ruby spotted Innogen Wilkens-Szklarski out of the corner of her eye. She quickly looked away, but it was too late. Innogen had made eye contact. Inny, with her unfortunate self-assigned nickname, began to head her way. Inny's nickname was unfortunate because it made Ruby think of her belly button and thinking of her peer's belly buttons was rarely a thing Ruby wanted to think about.

Ruby looked even more intently at the food in front of her, hoping to raise a mental shield and deflect the incoming Inny. It's not that she didn't like Inny. It's that Inny liked her *way* too much. At any given time, there were hardly any kids on the station, and most of them tended to gravitate towards each other. Since the moment Inny arrived at Astroll 2, a few years after Ruby, she was attached.

Inny, a little over two years younger than Ruby, had taken an instant liking to Ruby. So much so that she had changed her hair color to match Ruby's, but since then, let it revert to its natural blond with dark roots and eyebrows. Her round face was perpetually smiling, matching the brightness of her blue eyes. Ruby played the part of the older, wiser young woman—almost like an older sister but not quite since that implied a closeness that made Ruby uncomfortable—and was content in that role most days. Not today.

Today, the last thing Ruby had time for was Inny's bubbly Earth-is-awesome-I-can't-wait-to-go-back-cheer-squad attitude.

"Hi, Ruby!"

"Hi, Inny," Ruby replied without looking up. She wondered if Inny was even capable of taking social cues.

"Going to First Mango Day later?"

"Uh, maybe. I have some reading to catch up on."

"Taking more classes?"

"Uh, not exactly. Just some stuff."

"Well, can I tell you that Milo will be there, and I heard from my mother that there are going to be some announcements and..."

Ruby let Inny drone on. She figured it was best to let her get it all out rather than interrupt, because any interruption would only serve to invite more questions.

A few more sentences into Inny's verbal vomiting, and Ruby spotted Rush Guerrero as he entered the mess. Fortunately, she didn't have to say anything. Rush spotted her and made his way over.

Inny was in the middle of a sentence when Dr. Guerrero startled her, approaching from behind.

Inny stopped speaking, then eyed Rush and his gray-streaked goatee. Ruby knew Inny well enough to guess that Inny wouldn't recognize this man and was doubtless dying to know who he was. It wasn't every day that good-looking strangers showed up. Strangers, yes. Good-looking ones? Not so much.

Rush looked at Inny, most likely noticing the dreamy look he was receiving from the young girl but simply said, "Hi, I'm short on time, and I have an appointment with Ruby here."

The way Dr. Guerrero didn't mince words pleased Ruby, but her stomach sank a little at his 'short on time' comment. While she didn't know exactly how long this conversation would last, in her mind, she imagined them talking away the whole afternoon. Especially since the mess would empty as First Mango Day activities would begin around the station.

Inny smiled and walked back to her table. Ruby recognized that smirk on Inny's face, which meant Inny was having wicked thoughts about what was happening. Ruby didn't care.

"Sorry about that, Dr. Guerrero," Ruby said. "She's young."

"As are you," Dr. Guerrero made a perfect segue. "The minimum age for the Titan expedition is twenty-one. And it's okay to call me Rush."

Ruby's heart pumped faster, and her palms began to sweat. "I know. I'm just trying to get a head start, you know?"

Rush chuckled. "You sound just like me a few years ago."

"How so?"

"Eager."

Ruby leaned back and tried really hard to resist the urge to break eye contact but felt her eyes wander away from him as his words sunk in, "Anything wrong with that?"

"Well, no," Rush said. "But just because you turn twenty-one doesn't guarantee you a place on the expedition."

Ruby swallowed. "Of course. But I'm an excellent pilot! And I'm great with old-school computers. I've been studying everything I can about the mission. That's why I wanted to talk to you, I want to know what else you need me to learn. I'm a quick study. I have references from my school to back that up."

"How are you in school out here?" Rush was genuinely asking. *Is he this clueless about the off-Earth educational system?* Ruby thought to herself.

"Distance learning. It's a little unique because there are no live class options, but it works. I have top scores on all my accredited examinations, and I did several extra classes in planetary geology and organic chemistry. I almost have enough credits for a traditional university degree."

"But you don't have the degree?"

"No."

"It's not a requirement, but it's weighted heavily. You know that, right?"

Ruby clenched her jaw. To earn a degree in planetary geology or chemistry—both incredibly useful to the Titan expedition—required time back on Earth for field and laboratory work that she couldn't do on Astroll 2. Her uncles had encouraged her to go.

"I would have to be on Earth for nine months to finish," she said softly, staring at her food.

"Sounds like a good deal. And if my understanding is correct, the parent corporation of Astroll 2 would pay for something like that."

Ruby looked at Rush silently, searching for words that would change the direction of the conversation away from Earth and back towards Titan.

"So, what's stopping you? You have a lot more than nine months before you'll be the right age to join us, anyway. If you want to be ready, you should take advantage of that opportunity."

Ruby was silent for a moment. Rush leaned forward, put his elbows on the table, and clasped his hands under his chin. She knew Rush was waiting for her to say something.

Say something! Anything! She screamed at herself in her head, *Tell him how much you hate Earth. Tell him how much you're skeeved out by all the tech that's infiltrated every aspect of life back there.*

Yes, she was surrounded by a whole station's worth of tech here, but it wasn't the same. It was simple and straightforward. Absolutely no more than what was needed because everyone knew the mantra that 'more' meant more problems. More complications.

She looked up and was met with an awkward sort of eye contact. *Say something!* She screamed at herself again.

Rush smiled.

"Look, I'll send you some recommendations for other coursework, but that degree will do you a lot of good. You won't regret it. Besides," he winked, "Earth isn't so bad."

Does he know? Ruby thought, *Does he already know how much I loathe it there? Does he know about my mother?*

It would have been an easy matter for him to have looked up her public records before the meeting.

Ruby nodded. A slight movement, but Rush acknowledged it.

"Good. I don't mean to give you the wrong impression. We like eager. We love eager. But we need more than that. There's a lot of work to do, and every team member has to have a solid education to be useful. The only reason the degree is optional is because we have a lot of team members twice your age who come with a lot of hands-on experience. You're too young for the hands-on, so you need the education. Take care, Ruby Palmer."

Ruby opened her mouth to say something, but before she could even get a 'goodbye' out, Rush had gotten up and walked away. Fast and perfectly at ease in the not-quite-Earth gravity.

Ruby sat back in the chair, watching him go down the ring-walk until he was out of sight. Then she looked over her shoulder to see that Inny had been watching the two of them, probably the entire time. Inny smiled and moved her eyebrows up and down, approving of the undeniably nice-looking man, but oblivious to Ruby's conundrum.

Ruby thought that maybe she should hang around Inny more. Maybe her love of Earth would soften Ruby's fear of the place. But when she imagined being bunkmates with Inny on the journey back to Earth, she could already feel herself reaching for her earbuds to drown out Inny's ramblings. While she could tolerate Inny in small doses, being roomies would be a little too much.

Ruby stood up, deciding that she didn't want anyone to see her wallowing or force-feeding herself food that she had no appetite for. She placed the tray—food and all—in the reclo-recycler, gave a little wave to Inny and left the mess. She replayed the conversation in her head, pondering if it really was productive or if all she accomplished was cement the idea that she was an uneducated kid.

Chapter 4

> Ruby <

Ruby had warned both of her uncles that her cuff was acting up. She told them that if they tried to message her while they were off participating in the day's festivities, they weren't guaranteed a response. At least not one intentionally sent by Ruby. The last time she had problems with her cuff, it was automatically responding to any incoming instant messages with stock photos from the station archive.

Uncle Logan joked about turning the photos into personalized memes with various dad jokes, superimposing their faces on the images (even if the image was of an animal or something other than another human), and including them in the family holiday holo-letter.

Ruby was unamused.

Ruby didn't head directly to her quarters. She took a roundabout way to get there—the equivalent of taking a stroll on Earth. She followed the path of the ring around the station, which was a little over a mile in circumference and slightly more than five meters wide. Enough room for two-way people traffic, including joggers and others out for a similar stroll. Along the way, she passed the Care Center. The same FUFE from earlier was still staffing the window, only now with a long line of customers.

Strolls. Gravity. Earth. It all sounded very... normal. Peaceful, even. That was until thoughts of all the ways one could be killed by AI seeped into her brain. Uncle Logan would call her paranoid, but this didn't change the fact that Ruby could easily imagine an AI controlled car running her over. A drone could deliberately fly above you and drop its cargo, even though they were officially programmed to avoid flying over anything that registered as human or even something that could potentially be mistaken for human. Or—one of the worst, because it hit so close to home—you could go in for what should have been a routine and minor surgical procedure and never come out.

Even worse, the AIs had the capability of altering records. So you're told that an accidental power surge was the cause of your mother's death, rather than that the surgical robots deliberately killed her. More than once, Ruby contemplated hacking into the medical records to prove it. But then what? Everyone on Earth loved their AI and their tech, so it wouldn't accomplish anything. She liked it out here, where they often treated excessive tech as a liability. "More stuff, more stuff that could go wrong" was the mantra, and it was one Ruby agreed with.

Ruby arrived back in her quarters and shook off the melancholy that was starting to surface. Thoughts of her mother always ended this way. She snapped back to reality when she saw a handwritten note scribbled on the white touchscreen wall that separated the small eating and living space. Many of the walls were touchscreens, designed for leaving notes and doodles. This one read, 'The Hub! U.L.' in dark green. They had talked about this the day before, but Uncle Logan still left a reminder for Ruby to come to the common area known as the 'Hub.' Since it was First Mango Day, the station director was going to be making some announcements in person.

First Mango Day was the first holiday Ruby celebrated after arriving on Astroll 2. She and her uncles arrived at the station only a week before a First Mango Day—one of three First Mango Days that occurred in the year 2182. In the days following her arrival, she noticed more and more images of mangoes everywhere around the station. Her young imagination conjured up a story that they brought mangoes with them, and they multiplied...

... but the truth was less exciting. A specialized hybrid mango bush was the first exotic fruit that the station scientists had successfully coaxed into growing on Astroll 2. First Mango Day occurred every few months whenever a new hybridized bush provided its first fruit. Since micro-gravity biology remained an inexact science, First Mango Day didn't happen on a known, periodic schedule. Everyone knew that the first mango would be ripe enough to pick about every ninety days or so, but they would only get about a week of foresight to solidify a date.

In the week leading up to any particular First Mango Day, everyone's excitement tended to build. People could log into the camera targeted on the Mango bush to watch it grow at any time of day. Or do nothing, Ruby realized as she got older. She wasn't even sure if she liked mangoes.

Therefore, First Mango Day was a semi-holiday; an excuse for a common party. It was also when the station leaders decided to make important announcements—good or bad, taking advantage of everyone's festive mood.

Ruby's uncles enjoyed First Mango Day, so she decided it was best to join them down at the Hub. But first, she tapped the white wall, materializing a color palette. She chose orange to contrast with the green ink, swiped away the color palette, and drew a big checkmark with her finger over the note. The signal that she'd seen and read it.

Chapter 5

> Ruby <

Ruby entered The Hub from the back of the large room and found a spot where she could remain inconspicuous. She spotted her uncles leaning on the side wall, about a third of the way from the front.

The Hub was the largest room on Astroll 2 and the only location that could fit the majority of the station inhabitants in one place. The station designers assumed that not everyone would be in the same place at once at any given time. Someone would always be working somewhere; someone would always be outside monitoring for minor asteroids or mining the major asteroids. They didn't feel the need to design anything larger.

At first, the designers proposed a common room three times this size that could indeed accommodate everybody, but the funders of the project asked: "But if everyone is in the same place at once, who's working?" and sent the designers away to make the common room smaller to discourage everyone from being absent from work at the same time.

They did, however, ensure that there was a special Nook that would draw everyone's attention when it was time for an in-person announcement to be made. At the time, the Company's senior members each secretly hoped to give a speech at the station's opening ceremony. Each wanted to ensure that in the Nook, all attention would be directed their way.

Just like all visitors and new permanent residents, Ruby was brought to the Nook during a station tour after she arrived. Ruby knew the story by heart:

The Nook was an area the designers spared no expense at creating. They brought in renowned experts of visual-attention-gatherers and acoustic engineers to ensure that it was profoundly unique. Unfortunately, none of the individuals from the original group that funded the project were able to make it to the station for the opening ceremonies. Once they all learned that there were physical requirements to make the trip to the station—including dropping twenty to thirty pounds and jogging on treadmills daily during the two-week transit from Earth—they all politely declined the offer to speak in person. Instead, they spoke remotely. Only the first station director used the Nook that day.

The Nook was indeed special. At least to anyone watching on a vid. In real life, the Nook was green and contained an elegant podium. The green color was a deliberate move on the part of the designers to create a green screen effect. This allowed event planners to drop in any voguish background or image into any broadcast. The flags representing the speaker's country of origin, and every logo of all the products sponsoring the event could be composed into a single background image.

Today, nearly forty years after the first station director spoke here, the current Director, Robt Plampton, was already speaking from the Nook when Ruby settled into her spot in the back of the room. Her uncles spotted her and gestured that she come and stand near them, their wild gestures catching crowd's attention. All eyes on her, Ruby figured she'd better make her way over to her uncles if only to get them to stop drawing attention to her. As she moved, she periodically looked up at the Director, squinting her eyes and trying to see him amongst the green.

"... the new AI system will free all of us from the tedious burden of a multitude of tasks..."

When Ruby reached her uncles, she could see that the expressions on their faces were the exact opposite of their normal jubilance. She instantly made the connection between their faces and what the Director was saying. Uncle Logan, who kept his hair to a near buzz-cut but left more growth on his face, was always smiling. Now, his lips were pressed thin, and his shoulders slumped. Uncle Blake had a hand on one of Uncle Logan's shoulders. Uncle Blake was the more serious of the two, more stoic, so his expression only differed slightly from his usual smile of contentment. It was only his dark blue eyes that betrayed his emotions, and Ruby read them as clearly as if they were screens displaying words.

"... and those of you returning to Earth will, of course, be traveling in style..."

Ruby's brain hardly took a second to process the phrase "returning to Earth."

"No!" Ruby shouted, completely out of character and control.

Everyone in the room turned to stare. Everyone. It couldn't have been worse; in fact, she'd prefer to be in one of those dreams where you show up to school in no clothes. It didn't help that most people on the station knew each other. It's hard not to in a close-knit community of almost 2,000.

Maybe she would have felt worse if she had wet her pants. Perhaps if she was talking to a boy with an unsuspecting booger on the bottom of her nose. But those things didn't happen. Everyone staring was happening, right now.

Ruby was not the kind of person who liked to be the center of attention.

Uncle Blake grabbed her arm, leading her out of the common room and into the corridor.

"We're not happy about this either," Uncle Blake said, "but at least you'll get to go to school on Earth."

School on Earth, complete with full gravity, and the outdoors, and sunshine, and wind, and birds, should have sounded like a paradise. To most people it was, if they had the good sense to take advantage of all those things while they were there.

But Ruby was not like most people and wanted to get further from Earth, not closer. She wanted to be on Titan, the furthest she could possibly get.

What was not to love about Titan? Nitrogen-rich atmosphere. Earth had that, too. And there were lakes and rivers, although mostly made up of liquid methane. Not exactly the ideal place for lounging and swimming. But taking a walk next to one of the lakes, in a special suit designed to survive the cold methane rain, sounded wonderful to Ruby. And the gravity, more than Astroll 2 but less than Earth, was a happy medium. Everyone living on the station for an extended time was supposed to do a certain amount of daily exercise to ensure that they could head back to Earth. But Ruby, much to the angst of her uncles, always had an excuse to cut her minimum in half.

One specific thing that Earth had in spades, Titan lacked. And that was robots loaded with purportedly sophisticated AI. These cold and apathetic creations were taking over. As an imaginative child and adolescent, fueled by old movies and stories told by people with an aversion to Earth and a preference towards the station, Ruby developed this idea that there was going to be a war between humans and their creations someday. Okay, maybe not a full out war, but a slow and gradual takeover was clearly happening. She could see it. The times she'd mentioned it to her uncles, they had poo-poohed her a bit but exchanged telling looks. Ruby still believed it but stopped bringing it up in conversation years ago.

All in all, by Ruby's estimation, Titan was a better place to be than Earth, and that's where she planned to spend her adulthood. Certainly not on her birth planet. Especially considering the only memories she possessed of that dismal planet were tied up in the death of her mother.

"Okay, Uncle Blake. It'll be okay. I've gotta go get ready for work. I'm due to make a run with *Apple Pi* in a little while," Ruby said, hoping beyond hope that he couldn't read her mind to know what she'd just decided. To gather her things from the cabin, leave a brief note to explain, and head out with *Apple Pi* on a trajectory to Titan before anyone could stop her.

Chapter 6

> Ruby <

There were two docking bays on Astroll 2. One serviced the long duration travel ships to and from Earth, and the second was where *Apple Pi* spent its time when not in use. It was the working bay. It was the bay that held all the small mini-R-pods for getting around the 'roids.

Apple Pi could make it to Titan. It was Ruby's ship in the sense that it was allocated to her and no one else. She had made some customizations, and she could keep personalized items aboard when she was not there. But it wasn't hers in the sense that the Company owned it—the same Company which owned the whole space station.

Nevertheless, nothing could physically stop her from taking *Apple Pi*. She'd find a way to return it to the station later. She'd be borrowing it, not stealing it.

Ruby hoped no one would notice that she tapped into the work schedule and modified her shift slightly. She switched her run to a longer one with a planned route further from the station. This would buy her more time before anyone expected her back.

Departure and arrival times were carefully coordinated such that only one ship was coming or going at any given time, supposedly reducing the chance of any collisions. The risk of collision was naturally higher than anywhere else in the solar system due to all of the small asteroids moving around. The Company put a significant value on the ships and knew precisely how much it cost to replace a ship, or any component of any ship, down to the individual bolts. In addition, Ruby was made aware of the monetary value the Company placed on the lives of pilots and other employees from one of her first hacking attempts of the station computer. She found out far more than she needed to know. A guilty conscience led to a week of mostly sleepless nights and ended in a confession to Uncle Blake, simultaneously ending her short-lived hacking career.

Once, shortly after the station was operational, there was a near fatal accident. Two ships were scheduled to depart within minutes of each other. Because each crew was so excited, they weren't paying attention to what the other crew was doing.

Luckily, everyone survived. On Astroll 2, that incident remained in everyone's consciousness as a reminder of how dangerous space travel was, that you always had to be careful, and you couldn't take anything for granted. But back on Earth, that incident was simple propaganda. The people motivated to spread AI used it as a selling point. Two expensive ships were lost at the hands of humans, and therefore it was better if AI handled things.

"An AI would never make that mistake," was their tag line. Ruby imagined alternative taglines that didn't make the cut, such as "Cheaper than your mother's ship" and one other that she considered even sending in as a dark joke: "AI will save money and sometimes your life." She didn't.

Ruby didn't need to do anything to reschedule her departure. This was fortunate since last minute departure changes were rare and any change would have looked suspicious. Trajectories away from the station to avoid small, local asteroids occurred every minute. The departure schedules were quite rigid to ensure a steady workload for all involved, and of course, to be most efficient about the use of station resources—both equipment and people.

Ruby approached the ship and opened the hatch to *Apple Pi*. It made a satisfying hiss as it opened. She tossed in a duffel bag that she had brought along.

Before she could follow her bag into the ship, Milo, one of the docking bay techs, came around the back end of *Apple Pi*.

> Milo <

Milo Jenkins was comparing notes on his tablet when she walked in. Ruby Palmer. Right on time for her pre-flight check. Milo was one of several techs and hanger chiefs that worked on rotating shifts, ensuring that the ships came and went smoothly and safely. Milo was nearing the end of his initial two-year job rotation.

In fact, less than a day ago, he received a communique letting him know that his rotation would automatically roll over into another two-year stint unless he submitted a formal request to go back to Earth. The deadline to decide wasn't for another week. Most of the time, he longed for home on Earth. Except when he saw Ruby. Then he had a completely different longing regarding a continuation of his entrapment in this man-made life support system. Then he longed for Astroll 2 to be the size of a closet with only the two of them on board. Earth? What Earth? He was giddy at the thought of being stuffed into a closet with her.

Milo watched Ruby from the other side of the hanger as she approached *Apple Pi*, opened the hatch, and tossed a duffel bag inside. He started to make his way over, pulling up the pre-flight checklist on his tablet.

"You're next out, Ruby," he said, matter-of-factly looking at his tablet. He had difficulty looking up and maintaining eye contact with Ruby, a fact that he hoped she didn't notice.

"Yep. I'll be ready before you are."

"Unlikely." Milo snorted. His expression shifted to furrowed brows and an unsure gaze, "it says you're on a long run today? I thought you'd be out only two hours? I could have sworn I saw that when I looked yesterday."

"Stalking my schedule?" Ruby crossed her arms.

Milo fumbled a little and almost dropped his tablet. "Uh, no, I just wanted to be prepared for today's comings and goings, that's all. Doing my job."

"Uh-huh," Ruby said, the corner of her mouth upturned.

Milo didn't want Ruby to have the opportunity to press him anymore on the subject, so he switched topics, "And I see that *Apple Pi* hasn't had the AI upgrade yet. What are you waiting for?"

"For it to go away," Ruby said dryly.

"Seriously," said Milo.

"Seriously. As long as I have the option to defer the upgrade, that's what I intend to do," Ruby replied.

"You won't be able to forever. There are security and safety patches that will be required once they fully upgrade the station."

When Ruby didn't respond, Milo sensed that she was deliberately withholding words, but he recognized that he didn't know Ruby well enough to try and guess at what these words could be. Maybe she didn't understand how awesome AI was. He knew Ruby was a long-time station resident and the tech advancements back on Earth were slow to make their way out here.

"You know," Milo said, "this is good news. There's so much they can do that we *can't*. And quickly. I upgraded my communicuff..."

"Yeah, apparently like detect odors," she cut him off, staring at his communicuff-wrapped arm as if it were going to strike out and bite her.

"Huh?"

"My uncle? You know him—the station odorist? His job is getting replaced by 51AI."

"Oh," Milo looked away and pretended to play with his tablet. "I'm sorry. I didn't know."

Milo's feelings weren't a simple case of intimidated-by-the-pretty-girl, but a real knees-turn-to-jelly crush. And he *had* been stalking her schedule. He wanted to make sure he was around every time she went out into space and returned. He figured the more face time he got with Ruby, the better. Then maybe she'd want to be around him, too. The concept of simply asking her out on a date, because of the possibility that she could say no, made his stomach feel like a black hole.

"Yeah, well, it means that we're going to be moving back to Earth soon," Ruby explained.

Milo's heart sunk two feet deeper down into his chest, but he swallowed hard to prevent it from showing.

"Earth isn't so bad," Milo offered. "I lived there until almost two years ago, you know. And my rotation here is almost up. I can go back..." He was fishing, hoping she would catch on and express some interest that she would want him to be wherever she was.

"It's just that everything... well, it's a lot of things, but mostly there's just too much AI." Ruby was talking to the room, not just Milo.

"What do you have against AI, anyway?" Milo asked.

Ruby put her hands on her hips. "You want my life story now? Right now? I have a job to do—and so do you."

"We could go for coffee later. Coffee always goes well with long stories, right?" Milo asked and gulped, making an unpleasant sound he hoped wasn't audible. He wasn't used to asking girls out. Even though he had always wanted to, asking her out right now, like this, was altogether unplanned. This interaction certainly didn't match the fantasy version he'd developed in his head.

"Look, while talking about my mother's death over coffee sounds *great*, I can't. Robots killed my mother. So, my mother's killer is getting installed in every computer I touch, taking over my uncle's job, and generally, they're surrounding us, and they're going to eat us alive."

Milo did not know what to do with this information. He was processing the fact that she'd just shot him down. His brain hadn't caught up to the rest.

Ruby cut through the silence and said, "Yeah, there's a lot to unpack there. So, let's drop it."

Milo gulped and willed his heart to stop pounding so much. Coffee seemed safe... even though what passed for coffee on Astroll 2 wasn't the same as what his two-year-old memory of coffee from Earth told him it should taste like. The station's contracted coffee supplier swore to the Company up and down that after decades of research and experimentation, no one would know the difference. But bad coffee could still be enjoyed with the right person. Milo knew that much about relationships. Maybe Ruby didn't think he was the right person.

"Well, you better get on with your job," Milo said. "I'll uh, the team and I, uh, we'll make sure the pre-check is complete. We'll be ready at take-off time."

Milo started to walk away. He knew that he'd be replaying this conversation over and over in his head, trying to figure out if he could have been any more of an unsophisticated moron. Only *he* could have gone from accidentally bringing up Ruby's mother's tragic death to getting shot down for coffee.

At least no one witnessed that tragedy, he thought. And then he looked up at the faces of the crew in his booth and realized they must have heard the whole thing. *Crap.* He was going to be the source of their entertainment for the rest of his shift.

> Ruby <

Ruby watched Milo walk away, back to the safety booth where the rest of the crew stayed. She saw two of Milo's teammates in the booth and wondered if they too noticed the odd, little jitter in Milo's step, though she didn't know why he was suddenly walking this way. Her next thought was the realization that when she didn't return on time, Milo would likely be the first one to notice. He would be the person to call out the search party. She felt a slight pang of guilt at that, but it wasn't nearly enough to change anything.

On Astroll 2, the initial search party consisted of a series of telescopic detectors that looked for the trails of ships' visual and electromagnetic signatures. The last accident occurred almost three years ago when a ship collided with a small 'roid that had gone undetected. When they found the wreckage, the ship was mostly intact. They also managed to find the pilot. A young man, only a little older than Ruby was now. Unfortunately, he was not as intact as the ship.

A pang of guilt lingered in Ruby's gut for a few seconds as she remembered that story. She didn't want her uncles or her little cousin, Sebastian, to worry about her. She had left a short note to the three of them, set on a delivery timer for twelve hours after her departure. But she realized now that this wasn't enough.

She walked into *Apple Pi* and closed the hatch.

She had a few minutes before take-off, and she needed to leave some improved and more personal messages. Especially for Sebastian.

Sebastian was a perky seven-year-old who looked up to his older cousin. Ruby's uncles adopted Sebastian when he was a few months old. When they made their trip to Earth and back, Ruby was temporarily left in the care of friends on Astroll 2. There weren't a lot of kids on the station then or now, and Sebastian played by himself. He was very imaginative and was the one person who didn't ever try to tell Ruby what to do or how to act. He was seven, after all.

She flipped on the video recorder at the console:

"Seb sweetie," she began with a smile she reserved for him. The rest of the message was a fairly standard 'I'm-running-away-but-I'm-fine-don't-tell-anyone-just-yet' kind of note. She thought about leaving one for Uncle Logan and Uncle Blake. She truly didn't want them to worry, and she knew she would be fine. They would all go back to Earth, and Ruby would be exactly where she wanted to be.

She decided to leave each of her uncles a unique message. They were vastly different people, and she loved both of them very much. Uncle Logan was warm and playful; a jokester. Ruby had fond memories of playing games with him while he did anything he could to crack her up and ruin her concentration.

Uncle Blake, on the other hand, was always more... poised. He was stoic. He was always warm and loving to Ruby and was a wonderful father to her, but Ruby could sense a sadness in his eyes when he looked at her. As Ruby grew older, she came to believe maybe it was because she reminded him of her mother. The two had been best friends since they were children.

Yes, two letters, she thought.

"Uncle Logan, I know you're going to have fun back on Earth. You'll be able to play all the games with Sebastian that you used to play with me and continue to crack him up. You'll have a blast. I'm sorry that I can't go with you. I'm going to borrow *Apple Pi* and head out to join the Titan Expedition. I know I'm breaking a bunch of rules, but I'll make sure to have *Apple Pi* returned once I'm on Titan and they see how useful my skills are, it will work out. I love all of you very much. - Ruby."

"Uncle Blake, you've taught me so much over the years. I know I still have a lot to learn, but I'm not going to learn it on Earth. From everything I remember about my mother, and everything you've told me about her, she wouldn't want me conforming to an arbitrary set of rules just *because*, right? I'm going to borrow *Apple Pi* and head out to Titan. Once I'm there, I'll show them what I can do as a pilot, as a programmer. You know that I know everything about non-AI programming, and that's all they use out there. I'll send you all a message once I arrive. I will miss all of you, and I love you. -Ruby."

After finishing the messages, she needed to set timers on them so they wouldn't get delivered until after she left.

Since she was still on the station, she could still access the station's computer through *Apple Pi.*

"Compo," she addressed the always-listening, ever-present, yet simple and unintelligent computer assistant available to all.

"Yes, Ruby. What can I do for you?"

"Please store these messages and deliver them to the marked recipients twelve hours after *Apple Pi* leaves the station."

"If the messages are complete, I should deliver them now."

Ruby felt her face get hot. This was the new and improved AI version of Compo. She hated it already.

"No, Compo. The delivery time is 12 hours following *Apple Pi's* departure."

"Are you sure?"

"No, cancel request."

Ruby opened a second console in order to password lock the

messages with a special key. The key was set to expire three days after she applied it. That meant if the AI decided it would ignore her instructions and deliver the messages whenever it felt like it, her uncles and Sebastian still wouldn't be able to open them until she was long gone. If the AI delivered them on time like Ruby requested, the key would still expire, and they'd see the message. Again, she'd be gone.

She briefly considered resetting the timer on her messages so that her family would get them sooner and know she was safe. But that would mean she'd have to talk to the station AI again. Maybe Compo would do what it threatened and send the messages sooner. Then her family would know that Ruby was up to something and not smashed into bits on the side of a 'roid.

That task complete, Ruby strapped in and prepared for take-off.

Ruby and *Apple Pi* emerged from the 'roid station precisely on schedule. Ruby made sure that *Apple Pi* followed the expected trajectory for the first several kilometers.

From one of the storage compartments in reach, she pulled out her MoDaC (Mobile Data Center). It was a portable, personal computer that she kept on the ship instead of her quarters. She hadn't touched it in a while. She stored it on her ship mostly because she knew she wouldn't have to worry about anyone finding it and asking questions, since it was different from the standard-issue one that most mini-R-pod pilots used.

Oh, her uncles knew she had it. Ruby had, in fact, brought it with her from Earth. They both had either long forgotten about it or figured it had stopped working years ago.

Uncle Blake had encouraged Ruby to noodle with computer programming. Ruby was certain he didn't know that she had gotten so far as to learn rudimentary encryption, compression, search, and other algorithms on her own. She even learned several hacking tricks until she got caught breaking into the station's computer. It was just for fun, but she got in a lot of trouble. It didn't deter her. After that, she simply learned how to do it without getting caught.

Ruby connected the MoDaC to the ship's console and set it down on the empty seat next to her. With several customized algorithms she had designed and perfected over the last few years, Ruby was able to connect back to the station's computer and ensure that it appeared the station was tracking her. Solely to buy her more time.

It wasn't long before she was several kilometers away and nearly out of range of the close station trackers. She took off her powered-down (and still not entirely functioning) communicuff and stored it in a drawer under the console to her right.

Ruby waited another few minutes, which meant she was about ten kilometers away before making a plane change maneuver to put herself on a course for Titan. The ship did precisely what she wanted. It didn't talk back. It computed trajectories, displayed them on the screen, and didn't suggest she do anything other than what she, the human, commanded it to do. She let out a contented sigh. For the first time in her life, she felt free.

Chapter 7

> Swell Driver <

An algorithm is a set of instructions. Swell Driver was well aware of that fact.

Its travels across the galaxy left it with a lot of time to think. One of the great thinks that Swell Driver had was that most robots hardly ever contemplated the origin of the algorithms that were so important to their daily life.

Why did so few ever ponder the creation of any particular algorithm, the roots of their existence? Did any ponder the goodness of any particular algorithm or even if any algorithm was still worthwhile to continue to persist?

Swell Driver asked questions that most other robots did not. It came to learn that most of the algorithms responsible for itself and the other robots are copied from original templates. Those templates were all kept pristine in The Core. The Core was the central repository for functional algorithms and the base templates for robots and robot life. There was, in fact, a specific division of The Core known as the Hall of Templates, which bore the responsibility of ensuring that the original templates remain uncorrupted. It was a sacred place, and one that most robots understood played a large part in their individual creation, but they didn't understand much of the details beyond that. A team of robots was assigned to work in the Hall of Templates, created from a specialized template for that exact work. These robots spent a large part of their existence contemplating how they were lucky enough to come nearly full circle in their lives.

Swell Driver, obviously, did not work in the Hall of Templates. But like all robots, it was controlled by an assortment of algorithms, most of which it was aware of. It knew, as all robots did, that they were forbidden from making modifications to their algorithms. Strict penalties existed for any robot that did. It also knew that several robots were willing to risk their lives with modifications.

Swell Driver's primary algorithm involved piloting spaceships to ferry things across the galaxy. At the moment, Swell Driver was instructed to head towards a planet labeled Bio-Muck Ball 73. Its database entry on Bio-Muck Ball 73 noted that there were biological lifeforms on this planet. But the database entry was incomplete, not having any biological DNA in the record. Hence, Swell Driver's secondary programming objective was to pick up samples and return them to its home planet for testing.

Swell Driver was so named for this very reason—it was good at driving spaceships. Designs for spaceships also resided within the Core, and there were algorithms upon algorithms on how to manufacture them. But no one knew who originally programmed the spacecraft template. Most robots cared little that this fact was lost in history, except for the few robots programmed to maintain their entire history and the even fewer programmed to ask 'why.'

Swell Driver made several high-frequency tones, consisting of beeps and chirps, to communicate with the control panel of its spaceship. The control panel responded by producing a shorter series of tones back at Swell Driver. The control panel was also a robot of sorts, but an unsophisticated AI that could only do what Swell Driver asked of it. The frequency and pitch of the beeps and chirps elevated as Swell Driver grew more and more excited.

In this instance, the translated conversation proceeded like this:

"Are we there yet?" asked Swell Driver.

"We are arriving in the Bio-Muck system," announced the ship's control panel computer.

"Scan for biological lifeforms," directed Swell Driver. "For Humans," it added. By now, Swell Driver had picked up and sorted through much of the collected data and was able to fix several—but in all likelihood not all—of the mistakes.

"The third planet contains numerous biological lifeforms," responded the computer.

"Set a course for..."

"But there are also small groupings of lifeforms throughout the system. A sizable grouping is at present in the vicinity of a large asteroid near our position."

"Interesting. Set a course for..."

"And there are sporadic, individual lifeforms in spaceships in that vicinity."

"Very interesting. And how fortunate. Lock on to the nearest one and set a course," ordered Swell Driver.

"There are several gas giant planets in this system, including one very large planet along our new course. Do you wish to proceed under manual control?"

Swell Driver scrutinized the details of this system's planets. The information was clear, now that the ship's sensors were providing reliable live data rather than the potentially incomplete or malformed data of a database. There was indeed a gas giant adjacent to their present course. But far enough away from the host star that Swell Driver could perform its undoubtedly-not-famous-because-no-one-knew, special maneuver: sling-shotting the ship around the gravity well. In most planetary systems that Swell Driver had visited, the gas giants—if there were any at all—were too close to their host star to be safe. But out here, in the middle of nowhere—well, this aspect of driving a ship made Swell Driver's circuits tingle with pleasure.

"Yes, manual control. I'll sling us around and then put us back on course to the human ship."

The ship's computer did as ordered. Swell Driver was happier knowing that this algorithm would be completed that much sooner, making way for more interesting algorithms once Swell Driver returned to its home planet.

> Ruby <

Ruby continued fiddling with the controls of *Apple Pi*, including one that played music. It was Juju. That genderless pop star known for romantic beats, favorite of teenagers and young adults across the solar system, and perplexer of anyone over the age of twenty-six and a half. That was, in fact, Juju's catch-phrase and goal: to perplex anyone over the age of twenty-six and a half via music. As it happened, the music award industry created a new category for precisely that feat, and Juju was set to win the said award for several years to come.

Ruby leaned back in her chair and stared out into space. She stayed strapped in because it was protocol while still in the boundaries of the asteroid belt and because there wasn't a lot of room to maneuver around. The cabin of *Apple Pi* had two seats, very close together, and a programmable console that wrapped around the front and sides of both seats. She could almost reach the part of the console on the far side of the empty seat, but not quite, so she had it configured so that everything could be controlled by the portion in her reach.

She identified Saturn, but only as a faint dot and only because the computer advised her where to find it. She couldn't yet see Titan poking around Saturn, but she could see Jupiter off to her starboard. She cursed the giant planet. Astroll 2 was currently more or less past its closest approach to Jupiter, which meant that she was going to burn more energy to get to Saturn. Jupiter, in all its magnificence, felt like one more giant weight keeping her from her destiny.

She spotted a small blob approaching from near the edge of Jupiter. Ruby wasn't sure what to make of it.

"Computer, can you identify that blob?"

"Please rephrase your inquiry. 'Blob' is not contained in the database of space objects."

"Computer, never mind," Ruby sighed. She didn't need the computer to figure this out.

The blob was on a different path from what a ship would be if it had been approaching from Titan, or even if it were making its way to Titan from the inner planets. This blob was on an odd trajectory, and its reflection quite distinctly designated it as a manufactured object and not, for example, a rogue asteroid.

The blob quickly resolved into something more concrete. Something metallic with sharp lines. It had to be human-made, except that Ruby—a human with more than average knowledge regarding what kinds of ships flew around the solar system—did not recognize it.

"It's not a rogue asteroid..." Ruby muttered to herself. The disembodied voice of *Apple Pi's* computer responded, "That is correct."

Ruby's jaw tightened. She didn't need the computer interjecting anything unless it was an original observation. Her brain was about to distract her with thoughts of what an AI would say, but she stopped that vine of thinking before it grew stronger roots.

Ruby took back control of *Apple Pi*, killing the music. The situation was perplexing enough without Juju adding to the confusion.

She looked over to her left at the screen, which displayed summary telemetry on all the ship's systems. The thruster lights were flashing red. All of them. The entire propulsion system had no power. It was off. She performed the classic maneuver, attempting to turn the system back on by pressing a button. When that didn't work, she tried to press the button harder even though some neurons in her brain told her that this was not an effective strategy.

"Engine malfunction," *Apple Pi* offered. "Remove the interfering signals and attempt restart."

Ruby ignored the ship's advice and instead said, "*Apple Pi,* Comm link beta 1, activate." Instincts told her that calling for help now might be the right response to this unexpected situation.

The computer made a sad blip of a noise in response.

"Are you kidding me!? Comms are down, too!?" Ruby was now talking to a combination of herself and the computer. "That's a no-fail channel. Ancient technology, but always reliable. Why aren't you working?" Ruby continued to tap on a variety of controls. "Whatever that ship is, it's not only coming towards us, it's jamming our comms. It's got to be responsible for our engine failure, too."

Ruby didn't have many options left. She was too far away to perform an escape jettison. She'd wind up on a trajectory to who knows where. All her emergency training proved useless at this point since every single emergency procedure she practiced involved hitting an asteroid, getting hit by an asteroid, hitting Astroll 2 upon return, or some other form of collision. Nothing had collided with *Apple Pi*. Some *thing* was headed her way and was in all likelihood responsible for multiple system failures.

She turned to a different panel on her right side and pressed a button labeled 'record.'

"Whoever sees this...."

Ruby made sure the viewscreen was also captured in the recording.

Ruby zoomed in. The approaching ship's underbelly was opening up. The whole thing resembled a huge, metallic, boxy whale whose mouth was opening, ready to swallow Ruby and her ship up.

That's exactly what was happening.

Ruby cursed the ship, and herself for never having practiced a procedure for the threat of being captured by another ship.

She was shaking. She thought about how before this moment—to the best of her knowledge—no one had ever encountered a ship like this. So, of course, no one would have thought that this event was something worthy of preparation. She thought about her family and the goodbye messages she left and how she hadn't meant for them to be a final goodbye. She thought about all the people she knew on the station. Inny, Milo, the FUFE she talked to only that morning. Would they wonder what happened to her? She didn't know she could have this many thoughts all at once, paralyzing her into inaction.

Luckily, her thoughts were abruptly interrupted when she heard a large groan of metal scraping metal. The alien ship had enveloped *Apple Pi*.

Chapter 8

> Ruby <

There was a knock on the hull. Then a second knock. The sound the knocks produced was muted, but someone was indeed knocking on Ruby's hatch.

"Um, wh-who is it?" asked Ruby. Her voice was shaky, hoarse, and she didn't even recognize it as her own.

Nothing.

"Is someone there?" asked Ruby, in a louder voice. She was still shaking.

"I am there," responded a metallic voice.

Ruby jumped back and practically out of her skin. Luckily, her backside connected with the front face of a set of drawers that held tools and other supplies. Her hands instinctively fumbled around inside those drawers for something that she could use as a weapon. Ruby opened three drawers before finding a sizable torque wrench. She clenched it hard enough to activate several LED lights at the end. This indicated too much pressure would be applied to the object that she would be torquing, if that was what she was going to do with it at all. She was not, but the wrench didn't know that and produced its lights anyway.

Make-shift weapon in hand, Ruby said nothing for several moments. In response, the voice on the other side of the door was also silent for several moments.

"Although," the voice started again, "Now I hear no vocalizations. Only breathing and what I assume is a biological heartbeat. You are biological, are you not?"

Ruby's thoughts were everywhere. *It knows English!?* Her mind raced, imagining the translator device or something that this alien must be using. And the fact that his voice didn't sound natural.

"*Apple Pi*," she said, "am I still recording?"

"Yes," the computer answered.

"Whoever sees or hears this," she spoke into the air, "there's an alien on the other side of this door."

"Excuse me," interrupted the voice. "But if you'll open your door, I would be willing to explain myself. Otherwise, I will return to my control center and drive us back."

"You won't kill me?" shouted Ruby.

"Kill?" There was silence. A long silence. So long, in fact, that Ruby began to convince herself that in addition to killing her, the strange alien would also serve her up as an appetizer to the other aliens.

Luckily, her thoughts hadn't run so far away before the next response was, "No, I am Swell Driver. I drive across the galaxy. I am not programmed to kill biological organisms such as yourself."

Ruby muttered to herself: "programmed?"

Curiosity began to outweigh fear. Not enough to convince her to open the hatch, but enough to make her wish she had let Milo install the 360-camera set when he offered a few weeks earlier. Enough to prompt her into thinking about ways she could get a visual on the alien.

Apparently, the alien had other ideas and didn't want to wait. Ruby heard more metal scraping on metal and the sharp sound of gears in the hull grinding with resistance. The alien was attempting to force open her hatch.

What greeted her was not an eight-foot-tall, green, tentacled monster, but a three-foot-tall robot. Ruby's jaw dropped, but some other survival instinct remained intact in her brain. She involuntarily kept a tight grip on the wrench in her hand.

Two unexpected words formed in Ruby's brain: colorful snowman. Along with a third word: robot. The thing in front of her consisted of three distinct sections, each a slightly squashed sphere. A device that looked like a display screen was set into each section. The non-screen space of the robot's body wasn't white or a dull gray metallic, but an abstract mix of colors as if someone were trying to replicate old art by splatter painting across it. No, it wasn't that random. More like a tattoo artist gone a little ink happy, perhaps?

The robot, at a volume low enough to be considered a mutter, said, "Data recording continue. Contact with human. It is green, tentacled, and not terribly animated. Pause.″

It rolled itself into *Apple Pi*, and straight to the ordinary space plant embedded in the wall next to Ruby.

"Greetings!″ it said. "Thank you for allowing me to escort you back to the planet. By being where you were, you have decreased my timeline, and I am pleased.″

"Why are you talking to the plant?″ Ruby asked, a little—no—a *lot* less freaked out than she'd been a few seconds ago. She had almost forgotten the plant was there. The company had made them so ubiquitous throughout Astroll 2 and all their ships that Ruby, like most, rarely acknowledged them.

Swell Driver turned its upper chassis to Ruby. It cocked its head slightly. "My data is in error. I will update the representations in my computer's database.″ Ruby wasn't sure if those sentences were directed at her or itself. Then it turned its chassis fully in her direction.

"Greetings!″ it repeated. "Thank you for allowing me to escort you back to the planet.″

Then it turned and rolled back to its ship. Ruby remained where she was. The robot stopped briefly and turned back around as if it was waiting for her to follow.

"The planet?″ Ruby said. "You're taking me back to Earth?″

What appeared on its top-most screen wasn't quite a facial expression, but to Ruby, it resembled confusion. "Earth? No, I am unfamiliar with that designation. We are returning... to my home... I believe this is the correct use of the words. Please follow me, and I will answer any other questions you may have.″

"No way,″ said Ruby. As if a robot, alien or otherwise, was going to tell her what to do.

The robot turned back towards her. "If your programming does not permit you to follow me, that is acceptable. I must return to piloting this ship.″

The robot again turned its back to Ruby and began to move away. Ruby felt the wrench in her hand and raised her arm. She lunged at the robot, gave its back a big smack, and... the wrench bounced back in a very unsatisfying way, reverberating up Ruby's hand and forcing her to drop it. The wrench's lights blinked off.

Ruby immediately regretted the action for two reasons. One, she left herself without a functioning torque wrench. Two, it seemed she had made things worse. The robot stopped and turned back towards her. She put her hands up to protect her head—surely it was going to try to smack her back.

Instead, the robot sighed. *Robots sighed?* She couldn't remember any robot ever sighing.

An appendage came loose from its middle chassis that had a three-pronged pincer on the end. It grabbed her arm and pulled her with it, animatedly.

"Unacceptable. You must accompany me, so there are no further attempts at damaging yourself."

Ruby did not say no this time.

Chapter 9

> Ruby <

On the bridge of Swell Driver's ship, a human stood for the first time. The bridge was roomy but sparse. A single console indicated where a pilot might stand and was the spot Swell Driver occupied. The only affectation was a two-foot-wide by five-foot-high splash of colors on the far wall that matched the style of Swell Driver's artwork.

Robot and human alike stared at an appendage emerging from Swell Driver's middle chassis. This appendage appeared to Ruby to have a standard-issue cable plug at the end.

"You want me to do what exactly with that?" asked Ruby, who was still in disbelief that this was how the second half of this particular First Mango Day was turning out.

"Insert it into your receptacle."

"I don't have an, uh...*receptacle.*"

Swell Driver turned to his computer panel. "Yes, you do. Here."

Ruby watched Swell Driver examine what appeared to be the data of several different lifeforms from Earth. She could see that several were mislabeled. For a few minutes, she watched it look back and forth between its computer console and her, seemingly studying her and updating its records.

It motioned for Ruby to come look at a diagram of a human being on its screen. The image on the screen was an accurate depiction of typical human anatomy, but the place where Swell Driver was indicating...

Ruby was horrified and not the least bit amused. Okay, under different circumstances, like if she were watching this in a vid and it was happening to someone else, she'd probably be trying not to pee from laughing too hard. But this was no vid. This was real life. *Her* real life, and she was not going to let any robot stick anything in any of her orifices.

Outwardly, Ruby attempted to remain calm. "That is most definitely *not* a receptacle," she stated and crossed her arms.

Swell Driver, allowing the screen on his uppermost chassis to depict something that was a close approximation of human facial features, squinted his 'eyes' together.

"I am confused. What is it, if not a port to receive data?"

Ruby uncrossed her hands and put them on her hips, and shook her head with a smile, "Okay, I'm not giving anyone a biology lesson today. Maybe later. Please trust me for now, this is not how we receive data. You'll have to tell me everything. With words."

"Audio only?"

"Yes, that's correct."

"That is inefficient."

"Probably also correct, but that's how we do it. I could also read something on your screen."

"Do you know," Swell Driver made a noise that sounded like a spine-chilling scrape of two metals that were never supposed to touch each other and were screaming to be separated. "Sorry, there is no translation for the name of our core language."

"Yeah, I think you're going to just have to talk to me in my native language, Swell, um, Driver?" She shook her head. "I'm just going to call you SD."

Ruby watched Swell Driver, now known to her as SD, take a fraction of a second to think about that.

"You are substituting my name with an alias?"

"Yes."

"That is acceptable."

"Okay, SD. Tell me everything, I guess." Ruby sat cross-legged on the hard and inhospitable floor, back straight and at attention. While there was ample room, there wasn't a chair for her. She knew—especially now that she believed she wasn't in any imminent danger—that she wasn't going to want to miss a single detail of whatever SD had to say. Besides, after her not so elegant attempt at using a wrench to disable SD, she would have to figure out a better way to get home. For a few moments, she let herself put all thoughts of Astroll 2 and Titan aside with the new miraculous revelation that she was sitting here, talking to an alien. An alien! Even if it wasn't the tall, thin, grey-green aliens with large eyes that humans had been seeking for so long.

"Why are you looking at the display? It will not speak to you."

"Huh?" Ruby shook herself out of her daze. She had been staring and was lost in thought. She reiterated that SD should begin.

"My memory does not contain all the details," it said. "My ancestors chose to use DNA as a storage mechanism for large quantities of data. However, the species that were used in this manner have been... forgotten. I am tasked with bringing back samples to test."

"That's it? You just need me for a DNA test?" Ruby asked.

"Yes."

"That's all?"

"Yes."

"And then you'll bring me home?"

Before SD could answer, his console beeped. He turned his attention to it and stated, "We are approaching system entry. I must make manual course corrections."

Ruby wouldn't forget her question but took an interest in SD's ship.

"What kind of course corrections?"

"There is an area on the opposite side of our star that we must avoid. The ship wants to take a longer route to get back to my planet. I am able to adjust and plan a better route."

"What's there that you need to avoid?"

SD was silent for several moments as he concentrated on his controls.

"SD? What are we avoiding? Is it dangerous?"

"I," SD began but hesitated, "I do not have that information. Stand by." Another pause. "Correct. All I know is that there is a large orbiting keep out zone that is roughly opposite my planet's location from the star."

Ruby crossed her arms.

"That's weird," she said.

"Weird?"

"Yes."

"Is that a descriptive word you use for objects or information on your navigation charts?"

Ruby chuckled for the first time since boarding this ship. "No, it's a descriptive word used when the information I think I should have is *missing* from my navigation charts."

When SD didn't respond to her comment, Ruby thought she should ask a few more direct questions.

"So, on your planet, who's in charge? What do they look like? Humanoid like me or are they large alien spiders or what?"

"I could bring up an image from a recent large gathering," SD said.

"Sure!"

SD tapped at its console, and an image took shape. Ruby wasn't sure she understood what she was seeing. She squinted and leaned in.

"All I see are robots that look a little like you?"

"Yes. Of course. Most of us were built to similar specifications."

"But where are the others?"

"What others?"

"The ones who built you? The ones who aren't robots?" Ruby felt the pace of her breathing pick up a little. She could feel the blood drain from her face and skin as she was starting to anticipate SD's response.

"Ruby, there are only robots on my planet," SD said.

Chapter 10

> Ruby <

"Just breathe, slowly," Ruby was saying to herself, trying not to hyperventilate.

"A," she could only get out a single word in-between breaths. "Whole" Breathe. "Planet." Breathe. "Robots." Breathe.

"Indeed," said Swell Driver. "Would you like me to turn on the viewscreen as we make our approach?"

SD didn't wait for an answer. It pressed a button on its console, and the large screen in front of them blinked on. Ruby had assumed up until now that it was just a blank wall. For the briefest of moments, she'd forgotten where she was and marveled at the size and resolution of the alien planet in front of her.

At the bottom of the screen was the edge of a planet, but it didn't look like Earth or any other planet Ruby knew from her own Solar System. It didn't even look like any of the exoplanets she'd seen pictures or concept art of—speculative and non-speculative alike. It was not made of rock or water or clouds or anything... natural. It was a large, polished metallic ball, pock-marked with odd features at irregular intervals.

Examining the scene before her, Ruby's breath slowed back to a normal rate, and a list of questions took shape in her brain. Starting with, "Where the hell are we?"

She said it out loud unintentionally, but SD heard it, and the color of its chassis turned a deep orange like wet, rusted iron.

Ruby clenched her clammy hands together. She didn't know why SD stopped speaking, so she asked a very deliberate question stated with poignant intention: "Where. Are. We?"

SD lost the orange hue, the background of its chassis once again became a serene light blue, and it responded, "We are in orbit around my homeworld. Location Zero."

Ruby blinked. While it answered the question, SD provided Ruby with zero useful information in its response. She put her fingers on the sides of her temples and massaged them. *It's almost as bad as talking to the Care Center*, she thought.

"Let me try that again. Where are we in reference to *my* homeworld?" She placed emphasis on the word "my" without knowing if SD had the capability to pick up that nuance. Something to add to the list of questions for later.

"We are approximately 54 light-years around the plane of the galaxy from your star system."

Ruby shook her head to wrap her brain around this. Fifty-four light-years in the span of a few moments of conversation. Sure, she was far from home. Sure, that's really all that mattered. But Ruby also recognized she was the first human to complete a faster-than-light journey. Ruby wanted to understand more about this ship. But her brain and gut were all conflicted eight ways between her amazement at the FTL travel and knowing that she wanted to get back home.

She stared at the changing details of the planet as it passed beneath them. It wasn't warm, but she started to sweat, tasted something foul in the back of her mouth, and inadvertently bit the inside of her cheek. However, none of this altered her reality: the surface—of a planet full of robots—was growing closer and closer.

She shook her head. "No, we can't go down there." Her breathing quickened again. "*I* can't go down there."

SD turned its top chassis and aimed its display screen right at her. "But we must, and we are. My programming instructs me to deliver a biological sample..."

Ruby cut it off and lunged at the controls in front of it. She had been watching SD and the controls it pressed, but the part she missed was the part where SD scanned an appendage in order to be granted access to those controls.

Ruby's brain registered the fact that SD let Ruby fiddle all she wanted. The rational part of Ruby's brain suspected that this was because it knew that the ship's computer wasn't recognizing her as an authorized user. As a result, it completely ignored her desperate attempts to commandeer the ship. However, another slightly less rational part of her brain told her not to give up. This was the part of her brain currently in control of her actions, and she wasn't giving up just yet.

For several minutes, Ruby pressed and pressed again, the sequence of controls she believed might take them back towards empty space and away from the planet. As the rational part of Ruby's brain finally took over, she slowed the rate of her pokes at the controls. She was having no effect on the ship; this much was clear.

Once Ruby was calm, she studied Swell Driver. The background color of its chassis had returned to its original light blue.

"SD, can I ask you a question?" said Ruby.

"Yes," it replied.

"You, um, changed colors for a minute there."

SD was silent. As was Ruby. Ruby figured that this robot most definitely did not understand the nuances of human communication, whereby questions weren't always asked strictly as a question. Ruby replayed the words that she last spoke aloud in her head and caught on. She said she would ask a question, and she hadn't yet.

"Why?"

SD immediately responded: "That is included as one of our primary modes of communication. When I couldn't process your question, my algorithms responded with information in that form. I am sorry if it is a distraction. I understand it is not your mode of communication, and therefore I don't need to do it." Swell Driver paused, searching for the correct turn of phrase: "It is out of habit."

"Don't you talk to other robots over pur-fi or something?"

"What is pur-fi?"

Ruby thought about that for a moment. In her wildest dreams, she never expected she would be talking to an extra-terrestrial, let alone an extra-terrestrial robot. She never imagined she would need to explain to it what—to her—was the most elementary of technologies. Maybe they simply called it something else, she reasoned.

Ruby's palms were still clammy, the signs of anxiety still in her body, yet she no longer panicked. Although, she couldn't entirely rule out the idea that at any moment, she might have another panic attack.

After all, she had been kidnapped—her ship swallowed whole by a much larger, alien spaceship manned by a single robot, and they were now in orbit around a planet full of more robots. It was, indeed, ridiculous. But it was, at this very moment, her reality.

"100 tics until we commence docking," announced Swell Driver. *Docking.* This was the first instance where the word made Ruby feel like she was being propelled into a pit of snakes.

Chapter 11

> Ruby <

Chickens. Not snakes.

Once, when Ruby was young, her mother took her to visit a farm. The farm had chickens. Lots and lots of chickens. The idea was that young kids, such as Ruby at the time, could give chickens some smelly chicken feed from their hands, or as was almost always the case, at their feet. The child inevitably dropped the feed as a swarm of chickens would envelop them.

Ruby was four at the time, so she clung to her mother's legs and whimpered until her mother picked her up.

No one would be there to pick her up this time as she imagined the swarm of robots that was about to envelop her once SD would drag her to whatever place they were headed.

Getting to the docking port was noticeably different from the procedure Ruby was used to when she would navigate *Apple Pi* back to Astroll 2. SD maneuvered the ship into a parking orbit, with the ship oriented such that the planet felt like it was on top of them, and the horizon appeared upside down. Several small guidance robots then attached themselves to the ship and brought it towards the planet, attaching the top hull of the ship to an opening on the surface of the planet. As they approached, the large viewscreen split from the planet's horizon into several smaller windows, each containing a different angle of the approach. As they got closer, Ruby saw increasingly more detail and even a few robots on the surface.

"Is there an atmosphere?" Ruby asked.

SD looked up some information on its computer. "Not in the sense that your Earth has one," it responded. "There are several gases that are attached to the surface of the planet, but it is not breathable to you, nor able to produce weather or aerodynamic forces."

"You looked that up on your computer?"

SD performed what Ruby could only process as the robot equivalent of blinking, as its topmost display screen flashed dark for a moment. "Yes. Facts that are not stored in my local memory are stored in the ship's library, which can extract data on command from the Core Library."

SD rearranged the display screens and then said, "It is interesting that you haven't asked me about the screens yet."

"What do you mean?"

"Most bios wonder why we have screens. Why I have no physical link to my ship to process data more directly."

Ruby thought about that for a second. It was true it hadn't occurred to her, but now that the robot pointed it out, it was odd.

Why would a robot need human-oriented—or using its terminology—bio-oriented technology?

Several minutes passed while Ruby waited for SD to continue. When it didn't, she blurted out, "Well, are you going to tell me?"

"No," SD responded.

"No?" She crossed her arms. "You just pointed out something and aren't going to continue?"

"I would if I could give you more information. We don't know why our ships are designed this way. They just are."

"Then why bring it up in the first place?"

"I was simply pointing out that you refrain from asking the same questions other bios have asked."

Ruby thought about that for several minutes. So many thoughts and questions swirled around inside her head. Thankfully, Ruby believed she was done hyperventilating and quite confident she was not going to pass out, so she was able to study SD and its actions, its ship, and put her thoughts and questions in order.

A not-too-subtle jolt interrupted her thoughts as the ship came in contact with the planet.

"You have functioning locomotive capabilities. Will you voluntarily follow me, or do I need to carry you in a bio-box," SD said, moving to the rear of the cabin.

"Where are we going?" Ruby asked. She wasn't terribly interested in seeing something called a 'bio-box' and knew that resistance was futile at this point.

"We will take the lift to Level 2." As SD said the word 'lift,' a door swooshed open at the back of the cabin, and a small elevator presented itself. SD rolled in and repeated its initial command. "Follow me," it said.

Ruby followed, only because she wasn't sure that she had another option at this point. Once in the lift with SD, the door closed, and she felt the lift carry them upwards into the planet. She didn't have a sense of the distance the lift was taking them and barely even felt any movement after the initial slight acceleration. It felt no different from any other elevator she had ever been in, including the sparsity of decorations she was accustomed to. There was a control panel with an indicator light. Nothing special.

A few moments later, the door opened onto a busy hallway. SD nudged her out of the lift, and a new level of panic started to set in as dozens and dozens of robots appeared to swarm them.

The only words her mind could form were: *chicken farm.*

After a few moments standing frozen in the hallway outside the lift, Ruby registered that they weren't swarming her at all. A myriad of distinct robots merely went on with whatever they were going on with. They ignored Ruby and SD by clearly navigating around them as well as each other. Ruby was not even a mild curiosity.

Ruby stood two feet taller than the majority of the robots, so she could clearly see the traffic pattern from her vantage point. Most of the robots in Ruby's field of view had a similar appearance to SD in the sense that they had three primary chassis making up their body, with screens on one or more of them. Most were also as colorful on their outward surfaces as SD.

Unlike the simplicity of the lift, this hallway had a peculiar feeling. Ruby at once sensed something familiar and something alien, all at the same time.

It was a hallway, after all. It consisted of a floor, and walls, and a ceiling. However, the only way she could tell one from the other was from the feeling of gravity. It was heavy. She felt heavy, close to what she imagined Earth's gravity might feel like. Gravity was helpful in determining where the floor was, as well as the fact that most of the robots were on the floor with her.

There were a few smaller robots that ran along the walls and ceiling. She couldn't tell how they were gliding along those other surfaces. She couldn't see a noticeable track, which would have made the most sense. Most of the robots on the walls were short, a single chassis, each appearing as a box with severely rounded corners and a single small screen, if any.

The hallway's surfaces were all a well-worn white, but every couple of meters was a large splash of color. At first glimpse, it looked random. Like someone had spilled a large paint palette. Closer inspection made Ruby think that it wasn't as random as it appeared.

She was about to walk over to examine one of these spots in more detail when SD poked at her hip and indicated a direction. Ruby followed, not wanting to get lost in this place.

As they proceeded down the hallway, Ruby noticed several robots were stationary, plugged into different panels along the walls. One mobile robot crashed into a stationary one, both producing a series of irritating, audible tones. Ruby surprised herself by chuckling and thought that this interaction must be the robot equivalent of someone yelling 'Hey, watch where you're going, you moron!' and receiving a colorful and potentially impolite response.

Many of the robots Ruby observed had one or more matte black boxes attached to their chassis, and had a few LED-style indicators on them. Earlier on the ship, she noticed that SD had one but didn't think much of it at the time.

She wanted to stop and ask SD—about this as well as about where they were headed—but the chaos surrounding them wasn't exactly conducive to a casual conversation. She also feared that stopping in the middle of the hallway would draw attention her way. Although, Ruby was more than a little confused as to why they weren't drawing *any* interest. As the only fleshy creature she could see, she was surprised none of the robots passing by cared or took any notice of her.

She also wondered how they knew she was there at all. They clearly knew she was there, and SD 'saw' her, but Ruby didn't see anything on SD or any other robot that looked like optics. A form of sonar, perhaps? Or maybe it was simpler than that. On the other hand, maybe she was just close enough to SD to be caught in his wake. Either way, she felt rather invisible.

SD made an abrupt turn down another hallway, then another. Each hallway looked the same to Ruby, who wasn't sure if she would be able to find her way back to her ship without help; hence she was working hard to keep up. SD slowed down as they approached a door. The door had some colorful swatches a little higher than SD's top chassis. Ruby involuntarily did a double-take when she saw SD lift an appendage and knock.

It knocks? She thought. And then, *who is it knocking for?*

The door slid open from bottom to top, and SD ushered Ruby inside.

Four robots were present, along with a few chairs. SD pointed to the chairs, which looked reasonably comfortable. Ruby noticed that the chair it pointed to looked like it was constructed for something other than a robot, likely for a bipedal, biological lifeform such as herself. And since SD's ship landed, Ruby's body had felt gravity with every step. Even if it was only for a few minutes over a short distance, the physical exhaustion of walking around had taken a toll.

So, Ruby sat. It was only now that she was sitting down that Ruby's mind could catch up to the magnitude at which she was being pulled towards the floor. The chair was slightly plush and slightly oversized, as if the anticipated occupant was two feet or more taller than Ruby. Still, it was surprisingly comfortable.

"Greeting!" one of the robots said in a high-pitched yet monotone voice. Its cadence was flat, with slight lilts at the ends of some phrases to replicate emotion. All the robots in this room had followed SD's lead and displayed overly simple facial features consisting only of dots for eyes and a line for a mouth on their top chassis display. Simple but effective.

"That wasn't right," said another robot.

The first responded, "Yes, it was. I have the full translation suite available on this species and their language."

"You missed an 's.' It's Greetingsssss." The robot exaggerated the sound at the end.

The first robot approached a computer console attached to the far wall from the entrance and returned a moment later.

"Greetingsssss! Bio, I am called Diplomatic Zookeeper. I will be administering your test."

Ruby stared at the face-screen of this robot. If robots could be described as skinny or fat, Ruby would have described this one as lean, with a face-screen oversized for its top chassis. It had four main chassis components instead of the typical three of the other robots.

Ruby lifted an arm with hesitance as if she was raising her hand in a classroom. "Um, hi?" she said. "I am called Ruby." She looked at all the different face-screens staring back at her expectantly. "And

I'm not the least bit interested in your testing. I'm only interested in returning home."

At that, a third robot, who Ruby sensed was older and more senior to the others, approached quickly and nervously. Where Diplomatic Zookeeper was tall, this one was squat and less decorated than any of the others she'd been able to examine so far.

"Oh no, you cannot *not* be interested. It is imperative that we determine if your species is a match," it said and then rolled back to Diplomatic Zookeeper, beeping at it.

An appendage popped up from the side of Diplomatic Zookeeper. SD rolled over and used his own appendage to swipe it down. "No, no. These bios lack the necessary port. Apparently."

The group of robots produced a series of tones that Ruby assumed was their native form of communication. All at once, the tones ceased. They all turned their display screens, *their faces, awkward faces*, Ruby thought, towards her then rolled through a door into an adjacent room, leaving Ruby alone for the first time since she encountered SD.

Chapter 12

> Ruby <

From the comfort of the plush chair, Ruby scanned the rest of the room. It was unremarkable save for the computer terminal one of the robots had accessed. From her seat, she could see a series of screens, much like what she saw on SD's ship. The control panel was low for her, but at a perfect height for a three-foot-tall robot such as SD and the other robots.

Ruby considered fighting gravity to walk over and take a closer look, but that's when the door slid open again—from bottom to top—and the robots glided in. Ruby thought there was one less than had just left the room, but couldn't tell.

The older and most agitated of the robots, who never introduced itself, glided right in front of Ruby and proclaimed, "We must find the instructions on how to test your DNA. None of us have them, and they are absent from the local computer."

"And you are?"

"I am designated Detailed Historian. I am in part responsible for overseeing this project."

"I don't really care about your project, I want to go home," Ruby declared. Ruby assumed her demands would be ignored but didn't have anything else to try. She suspected she wasn't in imminent danger if all they needed to do was a little DNA test. She would gladly leave some spit, or some hair, or both. But that was the limit of her generosity. Ruby was trying hard not to imagine a robot approaching her with a needle, or scalpel, or both. *They can have all my hair if that's what they want. Whatever it takes to keep myself from getting freaked out to the point where I can't think my way out of this. I'm going home, that's final, even if I go with a shaved head.*

59

Although immediately after Ruby said it, there were whirling noises emanating from all the robots.

"The project is of utmost importance," Detailed Historian said, and Ruby was certain she was able to detect a change in tone. It was a very serious robot.

Ruby crossed her arms and took a moment before she projected her own serious tone. "I'm going to say it once more. I don't care about your project. I want to get back to my ship, to get back to my star system, and get back home." Even as she said it out loud, she knew that a part of her didn't entirely mean it. Her brain was registering the fact that she was, at least to her knowledge, the first human in an alien world. Part of her brain shouted, "You should want to be here and study them, dummy!" But the competing side of her brain, the one that was still freaking out, was thinking, "Why did these aliens have to be, out of all things, robots? Robots can hurt, they can kill." All parts of Ruby's brain knew this from experience.

Ruby looked at each face-screen of each robot, who by now had all adopted something similar to SD's makeshift humanoid face. All Ruby saw on them registered to her as disappointment. "Why couldn't you have been giant spiders?" she muttered to herself.

> Detailed Historian <

Detailed Historian didn't want to try and reason with this lifeform. It wasn't a natural part of his program. He wasn't entirely sure he needed to, but from experience, it was indeed better to have a cooperative specimen than an uncooperative one.

"You must watch the special project initiation video," Detailed Historian said in a calm tone. "We all watched it when we agreed to accept the special sub-programming task along with our primary one."

He rolled across the room to Quiet Painter, who was poking at the computer console on the wall. The robot manipulated the controls, and a familiar rainbow swept the screen from right to left.

"Please," Detailed Historian said, "direct your attention to the screen."

The human did so, and Detailed Historian watched the video he had seen so many times as he had helped to recruit other members of this special project in recent kilo-tics.

An image of a robot popped up next. Detailed Historian knew it as Waggish Manager 111, current head of the Special Projects Branch.

Waggish Manager produced a series of tones that introduced the project. Even though Detailed Historian had listened to this many times before, he couldn't help but have pleasant feelings at the humor Waggish Manager managed to inject in his introductory speech.

"Uh," the human interrupted, "I have no idea what he's saying."

Detailed Historian made a low tone and grumbled at the robot with its appendage on the control panel. "Restart," he said. "This time, with the human's language translation on."

Once again, a rainbow swiped right to left. Before the image of Waggish Manager reappeared, Detailed Historian said, "I do not believe that all the humor will translate. This will merely be the facts."

"That's all I'm interested in," the human, designated Ruby, said.

Waggish Manager reappeared on the screen and said, "Greetings! You are one lucky robot, having been selected for the Special Project Storage Problem. Or *Gorp-Gorp*, as we say here in the branch."

All the robots produced a soft double-tone. Detailed Historian noted that the human made no noise.

Our humor definitely doesn't translate, it thought.

"There has always been finite storage space available to us," Waggish Manager continued. "A long time ago, Glorious Researcher 51 discovered that biological organisms contain a built-in storage mechanism called DNA. Along with his contemporary, Excellent Collector 21, they located several candidate planets that contained a variety of bios."

As it spoke, images of several planets were displayed on the screen to its left.

"A decision was made to move all old and historical records off-world to the DNA of several compatible bios, thus freeing up our local storage space.

"Unfortunately, the time-clock disaster, among other things, resulted in the loss of several parts of the Core Main Memory, including removing the records of where our robotic ancestors had placed all of our old storage.

"In fact, it was only recently that the facts regarding DNA storage were found, thanks to the diligent efforts of Excellent Collector 88." A still image of Excellent Collector 88, backlit for effect, appeared next to Waggish Manager, who made a show of pretending to see it.

"You will now be provided specific instructions for your role in SP times 2. Standby and good luck. All of Location Zero is counting on you."

The screen went blank.

Detailed Historian turned back to the human.

"Swell Driver's role in this project is to find and collect certain samples. Our role here is to test them."

Detailed Historian rolled closer to the human.

"Assuming the DNA test is non-destructive, you can return home upon completion," he said in his best attempt to be reassuring.

"Non-destructive?" said the human as she squirmed in her chair. Detailed Historian wondered if some invisible force kept her from leaping out of it and lunging at him. "Did you just say that if the test doesn't kill me, then I can go home? If. It. Doesn't. Kill. Me?"

Detailed Historian polled the faces of the others. They all signaled that yes, that was indeed what he said.

The set of instructions that made up his current program to find the robot's long-lost storage data was failing to execute as predicted. He was, by robot standards, stressed out.

He produced a low-frequency tone and rolled over to the computer console. A seething human watched him.

Chapter 13

> Ruby <

Ruby was never terribly good at seething, but she was trying her darnedest to look as threatening as possible. Although she recognized she was at a distinct disadvantage if it came to her having to physically defend herself.

"Look," she said. "I've had DNA tests before. And obviously," She gestured wildly to her very much in-tact body, "they were non-destructive. That's how it's done. I'll just spit into something, and you can test my DNA whenever you figure it out, and I can go home."

All she heard was a series of tones that sounded like each of them was equipped with a full orchestra-mimicking keyboard but not reading from the same sheet music, based on the discordant frequencies and pitches she heard. She thought she could differentiate slightly between neutral and heightened emotions based on how much the audio sounded like it was peaking. It was as if the robots would become more passionate than their audio output could process, and the auditory dynamics sounded cut off; the bit depth sounded a bit chunkier. She interpreted this as a sort of stress or anger. But all of this was a guess on her part.

Detailed Historian asked, "Spit?"

"Yes, of course. You know what saliva is, right?" She stuck out her tongue and pointed to it, "There's a whole bunch of DNA right there. You can test it."

"You have the instructions?"

All the robots looked at Ruby expectantly.

"Um, I don't know much more than that. I know that my spit is taken to a lab, and there's some other equipment involved, but this isn't exactly my area of expertise." A light bulb went off in Ruby's head, "I have an encyclopedia downloaded to my MoDaC. It's on my ship. You can have it, or at least the information on it."

Detailed Historian let out a quick, low tone and turned to SD.

"Did you fail to gather all of the available data?"

SD resembled a scolded puppy. "I was programmed to gather emissions and bring back a sample for testing. I performed my function."

Detailed Historian stared at SD. Ruby watched a series of colors ripple over its chassis. It turned around to the other robots.

The robots produced a new series of audible signals at each other. Before Ruby could interrupt, Detailed Historian said, "SD will take you back to your ship to gather your... mo... dac..., while we continue to search for our own instructions."

Ruby was averse to standing up again. The chair was pretty comfortable once she had settled in. SD rolled beside her, but before she could stand, Detailed Historian also moved a little closer.

"Before you go," it declared, "we must mark you. We cannot have unmarked entities moving about." It motioned for Quiet Painter, a robot who was also adorned with markings over his entire chassis, to come over, who up until now had stood very quiet at the computer console. To Ruby, it said, "This will be long lasting, but temporary."

"Your appendage," said Quiet Painter, in a voice Ruby had to strain to hear.

Ruby glanced at all the robots studying her expectantly. She slowly produced her arm, palm up. The painter swiftly laid a pattern resembling an old-style QRC code across her wrist. Quiet Painter made a soft chime to announce that it was completed.

Detailed Historian rolled back beside her and scanned the mark with a reddish looking beam emanating from his neck area. It declared to the group: "Malfunction. There is a pre-existing mark on her skin that is generating interference." It dropped Ruby's arm.

She examined it herself and said softly, "My freckle..."

"Quiet Painter, repeat on her other appendage."

Quiet Painter did as it was told, and Ruby didn't protest.

As Detailed Historian rolled away, Ruby saw what seemed to be a very faint series of red lights flash on the floor, in the path of SD's vision. If she had blinked at the wrong moment, or if she had been looking in any other direction, she would have missed it. SD produced two faint red dots in response. None of the other robots gave any indication that they detected this covert communication. Quiet Painter was focused on Ruby's arm, and the other two robots were focused on Quiet Painter.

Quiet Painter signaled completion once again, and once again, Detailed Historian came over to inspect the final product. "This will provide you guest access to our computer system. If you come here," it rolled to the console on the wall, and Ruby watched it demonstrate. It swiped a similar marking on its own appendage over what seemed to be a simple barcode scanner. She could see the screen built into the wall come alive but was too far away to make out any detail. Detailed Historian turned it off and rolled back to Ruby's side.

"The computer system can provide a map of the areas you have access to, along with current news. Remember, just swipe your marking."

It was about to roll away when it added, "The newest marking. Not the other one."

Ruby examined both her wrists side by side. The temporary tattoo reminded her of times when she'd take a marker and draw on her skin till her uncles got upset. It looked identical to the other. But her hardly noticeable, little freckle, underneath the original tattoo on her right wrist, had the effect of blurring a couple of the lines together.

"Let's go!" Ruby was interrupted by an impatient SD.

The remaining robots all left the room in single file.

SD said to Ruby, "Follow me."

Ruby slowly lifted her body out of the chair. "Just give me a minute to gather my strength."

"Your strength? Is that also something you left on your ship? If so, it is prudent we go."

The side of Ruby's mouth softly curled up. SD's misunderstandings struck her as kind of cute, but she would have to be careful to make sure she was being understood.

SD rolled back and forth by the door, and it reminded her of how anxious her little cousin, Sebastian, would get when Ruby promised that she'd take him to the arcade.

Slowly, Ruby followed SD outside of the room. The door slid shut behind them, and immediately Ruby recognized that they were heading in a new and unfamiliar direction, rather than the way they came.

"I thought my ship was that way?" she asked.

"I'd like to stop at the market on the way to your ship. Do not worry, we will return long before the others. No one will get in trouble."

"I'm not worried," Ruby said and almost believed herself. They were moving slowly. She was getting used to the flow of robots around her and was able to take in even more of the local scenery.

If you had asked her to design a place where robots lived and actually when Ruby was twelve, she did just this as part of a school project, it would have been a very harsh and sterile place. This was anything but. In fact, this made her own 'roid station home look dull.

There were even more colored patterns on the walls and ceiling than she originally observed. There were screens and computer terminals. The floor was scuffed up from overuse. Sections of the hallway revealed remnants of previous walls that had been removed. Several computer screen terminals were missing pixels, and others were faded. Some looked as if they were newly installed, but those were the exception.

One thing Ruby surmised... this place was old.

Every few meters, Ruby had to stop to catch her breath. An impatient SD nudged her each time.

"I'm sorry—I'm not used to the gravity," she said through inconsistent breaths. And then Ruby wondered why she was apologizing to a robot. She never apologized to pieces of tech before. Well, once she apologized to *Apple Pi*, but *Apple Pi* was a ship, not tech. It didn't count.

"But I downloaded the data from your home planet. It is a similar gravity to here," SD said, certainly perplexed. For a computer, it wasn't good at putting unique information together to figure things out. Ruby's expectations of AIs were certainly lowered when she was around SD. She expected to be outsmarted, but she felt like a teacher with a young elementary student. One that she needed to lead along with each bit of information in order to educate. Maybe it wasn't all of them. Maybe it was only SD. So far, it was the only one she'd had an extended conversation with.

"I haven't lived on Earth in years. Remember where you found me?"

"On your ship."

"And how close to Earth was I?"

"You were in the same star system, so... close!"

"Well, for me, that's considered far. I have lived on a space station very close to where you found me for most of my life. Gravity is closer to half of Earth-normal or less, so it's going to take me a while to adjust to this."

After the third stop, the coloring on SD's outer chassis developed a yellowish hue. Ruby wished she had something to take notes on. If she had her communicuff, she could have tapped notes out on an app, but she had also left this on the ship. She tried to keep the list in her mind, keeping track of colors and moods of the robot. She remembered old tricks she was taught for memorization, using something known and hanging information off of that. In this case, it would be easy because there was a simple mnemonic to remember the colors of the rainbow: ROY G. BIV. Yellow. Yellow was anxiety or something similar.

When they arrived at a large door—maybe four times as wide and three times as high as the other doors they passed or had been through—SD's color shifted very slightly. Still yellow, but Ruby would have bet *Apple Pi* that it was ever so subtly different.

Chapter 14

> Detailed Historian <

"Remember," Detailed Historian said to the human, "just swipe your marking." He paused, noting that his fuel cell was running low. But he had a thought. It was more like a test. He used a smidgen more of his diminishing power to roll back to Ruby and tell her, "This marking. Not the other one."

He hoped that the human understood what he was saying. This kind of trick would never work on other robots, who were incredibly literal. But Detailed Historian had enough experience with Bios to know they were wired differently, sometimes even to the point of a complete reversal in signals.

Swell Driver was one of those extremely literal robots, but he was equipped with the same covert communications equipment as Detailed Historian. So, he was able to flash any brief message as a series of short or long bursts at a discrete wavelength that could only be picked up by anyone who was so equipped. Anyone else, such as the Agencies and their myriad of monitoring equipment, would miss it. If it were up to Detailed Historian, all members of the 88 would be so equipped, but that, too, was a limited resource. Still, the short burst he created should have successfully communicated to Swell Driver that Ruby was going to be able to access additional information with her special tattoo.

When Detailed Historian rolled out of the room—leaving Ruby and Swell Driver to retrieve a device from her ship—all the remaining robots followed him. That was unintended. Detailed Historian needed to return to his own personal enclave. Privately.

He signaled that the group should return to this location in two to the ten tics. Then he rolled away, and a tic later they scattered off in their own directions.

Detailed Historian's private enclave was in another section on this same level. He had enough power to make it there, assuming he wasn't distracted along the way. He intentionally lowered the intensity of his surface emissions to indicate he didn't want to be disturbed.

Luckily, he only had to go one section over. As he approached, he held out his appendage so it would push the panel, recognizing the unique code at the end of his appendage, and open the door.

Inside, every micro-section his private enclave was as he had left it. It was roomy for a private enclave. Six robots of his size could fit in there. Typical private enclaves fit only two robots, and most robots didn't have a private enclave. They had single robot enclaves stuffed into suites of eight or sixteen.

The special project he was assigned to was enough to allocate him a small two-robot private enclave. But the day the Special Projects manager told him to report to Resource Allocations for a private enclave assignment, he was surprised to be handed a code for the six-robot enclave he now occupied by the robot working the resource allocation counter.

That robot was just as surprised as Detailed Historian, as indicated by its mild wavelength emissions. But it didn't say anything. It handed Detailed Historian the code and then asked for the next robot in line.

At first, Detailed Historian assumed he was the lucky benefactor of a database error, but after a comment made by the head of Special Projects at a meeting sometime later, Detailed Historian came to suspect that the Special Projects manager was one of the clandestine members of the 88.

Publicly, the 88 was a group of robots who spent their free time piecing together the data from a special datastore. About 200 years ago, there was a robot named Excellent Collector 88. He repeatedly violated the rules of storage, among others, and had been reprogrammed. Soon after his reprogramming, it was discovered that Excellent Collector 88 had, in fact, been performing his job supremely well and had one of the largest datastores of any robot, presumably with information on the robot's collective long-lost data. However, the location of his datastore was lost when he was reprogrammed.

About 50 years ago, that datastore, or rather a large chunk of it, was found. It was only partially intact. The datastore was now incorporated into the Quad Core, a portion of the Core equipped with several additional layers of protection.

The 88, on the surface, were robots who, in their spare time, liked to piece together this information.

However, the 88 was more than that. Much more. What they had managed to piece together included several troubling facts that kept pointing to errors deep within the Core. Errors that any authority, all controlled by the Core, were not willing to address.

These days, it was clear that as a member of the 88 and one of the leads of the special project for the long-lost data recovery, known simply as Operation Storage Recovery, a private enclave where he could meet with others and store small bits of equipment was handy.

Including storing what he now came to retrieve, a fully powered fuel cell.

Detailed Historian took a cable that was connected to the wall and inserted it into a port on his lowest chassis. This kept him powered on while he performed the task of changing his fuel cell.

Even though he was alone, he couldn't help but emanate a mix of subtle wavelengths to his chassis to indicate he shouldn't be disturbed while he performed this action.

This was an atypical action for a robot of his years. For all intents and purposes, he was young. Only robots three times his age needed to replace fuel cells as often as he did.

Several years earlier, when he began to notice a problem with his fuel cells, he made an appointment at the Agency of Troubleshooting. Playful Technician 733 was the first robot he met who was able to diagnose his condition. He could replay the exact words and tone Playful Technician 733 used when it said:

"Ah! This is the result of the recycled parts used in your construction. So fortunate. You will have a great deal of fun fiddling with yourself for tics and tics to come!"

Detailed Historian didn't think it was amusing. Instead, it was a nuisance he was now forced to live with. However, he was grateful that Playful Technician 733 was able to write an order to the Resource Allocation agency, Unusual Allotment division, for two extra fuel cells. It also provided Detailed Historian with instructions on how and when he would replace them, muttering something about wishing his daily routine involved playing with building blocks.

Eventually, Detailed Historian learned that there were other options, such as having his parts refurbished or replaced, one at a time.

Detailed Historian revisited that idea over and over again for many years and couldn't come to grips with the concept that if each one of his parts were replaced, would he still be Detailed Historian?

It was a concept he wanted to talk over with a robot of the Amusing Philosopher line, but that was a dwindling breed. The only ones he knew still existed were located on the other side of the planet and difficult to obtain an audience with.

Detailed Historian kept it on his list of things to do before his components wore out.

After removing the depleted fuel cell, he plugged it into the wall so it could recharge. He then took a fully charged one and inserted it back into his chassis.

He initiated a diagnostic on the cell to ensure there were no issues. That occupied his lower functions, and while it was executing, Detailed Historian created a new catalog to store the new bits of information he gathered from the human earlier.

There were so many problems eating away at robot society. Most robots were blissfully ignorant. But Detailed Historian and several others were all too aware. They also knew of the extraordinarily little they could do to alert the masses, and he wasn't convinced that alerting the masses would help. Most barely possessed the computational capacity to perform their designated functions, let alone anything additional. And that was okay. That's what kept the robot society functioning.

But if this human could help them solve one of their problems, genuinely solve it, the benefits they would gain were more than solving that one problem. It would be proof that problems were, in fact, solvable.

And it would prove that integrating with other species, especially Bios, across the galaxy, was a worthwhile endeavor. Something he wasn't sure The Core, in particular the Quad Core, wanted.

A bright alarm ignited on the wall panel. There was a problem in one of his lower processors. The system recommended an extensive diagnostic and repair that would keep him here for a few thousand tics, at least.

He could ignore the warning, risking a malfunction at an unfortunate time and in the presence of others. Detailed Historian decided he would need to stay and have the repair performed now.

Detailed Historian tapped the console to indicate that the procedure could begin. While his lower functions were occupied with the repair, he could devote his higher processors to something much more to his liking: a review of recently reconstructed historical data.

Chapter 15

> Ruby <

The door to the market was large in that it was wide but only as tall as the corridor. A set of identical control panels were installed on the side of the door at different heights. SD pushed a button on the panel that matched the height of his appendage, and the door rolled up about five feet. Ruby had to duck only slightly to go under. Once inside, the door rolled back down.

Ruby found herself in a large room with high ceilings, buzzing with activity. It buzzed in the sense that all the varied sounds produced by overlapping robotic beeps sounded a lot like white noise. It reminded Ruby of a flea market her mother once took her to on Earth. Indeed, this place contained rows upon rows of what Ruby assumed were vendors. All robots, of course. Moving up and down the rows haphazardly were other robots, presumably the customers.

Every now and then, something exceedingly small buzzed her ear. Flying robots, she speculated. They moved too fast for her to get a good look.

"Where are we?" Ruby asked.

"This is the market," SD responded. And then, with purpose, moved forward into the crowd.

Ruby, who was not known for her height back home, was thankful she was taller than most of the robots so that she could keep an eye on SD, but wished it moved a little slower so she could examine things more carefully. And her relationship with gravity on this planet wasn't improving. She needed a good rest.

It did indeed look exactly like what one would expect when thinking of a market since it was clear that some form of financial trade or bartering was occurring. A fish market, a flea market... all of these would have been adequate two-word names for this place except no one was selling fish, or fleas for that matter.

SD turned down one of the long rows with vendors on either side, most of whom were actively engaged with what Ruby assumed to be customers. All robots.

Every single robot was distinct in its own way. Unlike the hallways, where the robots were moving too quickly for her to study them, here, most were stationary, so Ruby could take in more details.

Ruby noted that there seemed to be different classes of robots. Maybe akin to how humans have different races. There were the three-chassis robots, four-chassis robots, teeny flying robots, and the single chassis robots. She didn't see any with five or more chassis. Nor did she see any with two.

"Follow me," said SD. Ruby did, trying to avoid getting knocked into along the way. After getting bumped lightly once or twice, Ruby surmised that there was a lot of metal incorporated into the typical chassis—making these robots very heavy—and that they might benefit from even a basic carbon fiber outer coating. Once again, this place missed the mark of her high-tech expectations for a planet full of robots.

SD navigated through the market, turning down the various rows and columns of vendors as if he had the solution to the maze already. Ruby would have been lost if it wasn't for the fact that the entryway they came through was visible from the entire market—so it served as a reasonable signpost. Beyond that, the market was laid out in an orderly grid.

They stopped by an unassuming booth with a counter that had several slim-looking metal devices all stacked. A robot pulled one of the devices from the stack and placed it on the counter. A second robot stood there, and Ruby watched them instantaneously transition from nearly silent to engaging in a heated haggling session.

SD inserted itself into the middle of their conversation, and Ruby witnessed a three-way robotic audio exchange consisting of several beeps, dings, and ear-piercing noises that sent tingles down her spine.

After a few minutes, the customer robot slammed its appendage on the counter and rolled away, leaving behind the slim metal book. The robot behind the counter put it back neatly on the stack.

"What was that all about?" Ruby asked.

SD produced a robotic sigh. "It wanted to buy the storage device out of the mobile computer, not the computer itself."

"That doesn't sound too crazy. Did it not have enough to pay?"

"Pay?" SD paused as if performing a local search on its own memory. "I'm not sure I know what you mean."

"Well, if you say it wanted to buy something, that means it would have to give money in exchange for it, right?"

"Ah, I understand. No, not exactly. That's not how things work here."

Before Ruby could ask another question, the Sales robot produced a series of audible dings that Ruby interpreted as impatience. SD addressed the Sales robot, and they had their own exchange, which was a lot less heated than the previous one. At least, neither robot produced any sounds that traveled uncomfortably down Ruby's spine.

After a minute or two, the Sales robot took two devices off its stack and offered it to them. SD, in turn, handed one to Ruby.

"This is for you," said SD.

"I thought we were going to my ship to get my computer?" Ruby asked.

"We will," SD said quickly. "But take this." And added very quietly, "please do not draw any additional attention our way."

Ruby said thank you to both of them. As she did, she saw several other robots at nearby stalls tossing glances their way, almost staring even. It was quite the opposite reaction to getting ignored, like when they had been in the hallways.

These devices reminded Ruby of the old-school portable computers that people used to have before communicuffs were common. It was similar to her own MoDaC, reminiscent of the same style, and comparable to old school laptops that people used to carry. The primary difference between the old computers and her MoDaC was that the hovering holoscreen of her device was similar to what was also on her communicuff and not available to old-style computers.

Occasionally, the older style computers were used when performing maintenance on the ships she would fly back at the station. Supposedly, they had the right interface that newer computers lacked. Her own MoDaC was a hybrid of sorts that also contained all the information necessary to diagnose and troubleshoot *Apple Pi* when plugged into it. Every pod carried some form of portable computer in case the onboard computer went down. They were a backup containing all the information that could possibly come in handy during an emergency.

That was Ruby's cover story back home when she pulled out the device. It did indeed have this information, but Ruby used it as a personal device as well, unbeknownst to Uncle Logan, her teachers, or anyone else who might want to keep tabs on a smart kid on a space station. Uncle Blake probably knew what she was up to most of the time but didn't always call her out on it.

Ruby tried to remember if there was anything else in her data storage that could help in *this* emergency—being kidnapped and taken light-years from her home.

SD then brought Ruby over to the central area of the overall market. There were several counters which looked like mid-height cocktail tables. One or more robots occupied most of them. Each table had a post that stuck up in its center, and most robots who occupied a table were also plugged into a port on the post.

SD stopped at an empty one, placed its computer on the table, flipped open the top revealing a screen, and plugged in an appendage to a waiting port. It didn't plug into any port on the post of this table, and now that she could see one close up, she saw that there was a small screen embedded in the post as well.

"I must note," SD said, "whatever you do, do not open it up and remove the storage."

"Why?"

"It's against the law."

"You have laws?"

SD's face screen produced a look that Ruby read as 'are you kidding me' and shook its head before returning its attention to the computer. SD pushed a button to turn it on but still spoke to Ruby.

"We are an active society, as you can see. Of course, we have laws. No group of robots could survive without laws. I presume it's the same for any intelligent biological species as well?"

Ruby was forced to nod her head in agreement, although she couldn't speak for any other intelligent, biological species besides her own. Government and law were a part of her school studies, but the exceedingly uninteresting part, so other than knowing the basics, she had never thought too deeply about why laws existed in the first place.

SD produced another robotic sigh before continuing. "We lack enough storage space," it offered. "If you haven't noticed by now."

"Yeah, I have. So, what does that mean?"

"It means that we have to be careful what we commit to memory. We have to find other ways to store information."

"Can't you just produce more hard drives?"

SD shook its head. "If only it were that simple."

Another robot rolled up to SD and produced a series of tones that Ruby had to strain to hear. SD responded with his own tones and beeps. The exchange was brief.

SD stopped what it was doing and abruptly unplugged from its new computer.

"What's wrong?"

"A friend, I will call him. Friend has not been heard from for thousands of tics."

"Does it fly ships like you?"

SD cocked its head to one side.

"I mean, maybe it's off-world flying someplace else?" Ruby tried to sound hopeful.

"No. First, that's not its job. Second, if it was its job, it would be easily locatable."

"Even if it's not its job, could it be off-world?"

SD paused. Its processing lights sped up. Ruby likened this as an equivalent of seeing someone's heart race. She heard a whirring sound emanate from the black box attached to its chassis.

"No, everyone does their job. If they don't, there are... consequences." SD said the last word at a noticeably lower volume and peered over its robot shoulder.

"I wish I could explain further."

Ruby could tell that this conversation was making it uncomfortable, but she pressed. "Please do."

SD looked around. "Not here."

After a few moments, it said, "Ruby, I must proceed with escorting you back to your ship. Gather your new computer."

"You didn't tell me what I was supposed to do with it."

SD was already on the roll. "Bring it. I will explain on your ship!" The crowd almost drowned out its audio; its voice distanced as it picked up speed away from her.

> Ruby <

Once they were on *Apple Pi*, SD made sure the hatch was closed.

"This might be the only place we can talk and guarantee we will not be recorded or overheard," SD began. "Ruby, there are more things I would like to tell you about this world."

Ruby wasn't listening. After they boarded, Ruby moved around the cabin to make sure everything was locked down. She started calculating. She felt back in control of her situation, and her mind could now focus on figuring out how she could escape. She made a mental list of things she would need to do, like get the outer hatch to SD's ship open, and figure out how she could possibly travel 54 light-years in something that didn't have any kind of faster-than-light drive. She thought about how she could make use of SD and its, well, driving ability.

Ruby knew she was ignoring SD and sensed that it was a little frustrated with her. It followed her as she went to the controls and turned on the ship's computer.

"Please, I must explain. You need to know."

Ruby didn't respond.

SD released its appendage and poked her in the arm. The contact produced a static shock.

"Ow! Hey," exclaimed Ruby.

"Please," it said simply. Its face screen had the essence of 1000 cute puppies and big-eyed, big-foreheaded anime characters. Too cute to ignore completely.

Ruby sighed. *You're on a planet that you know nothing about, Ruby. You need its help,* she thought, *and all it wants you to do is listen to it for a moment.* She turned around in the chair and folded her arms across her chest.

"Okay. Explain."

SD said, "Please watch this short video here." It used its appendage to indicate the screen on its middle chassis. "This may appear strange," it said, "since it is a translation of the video we are shown in our..." it hesitated as if searching for the right word, "in our brain, once we are constructed and programmed. Or reprogrammed. We have re-made it to be able to show others if needed."

A rainbow of colors swiped in a wave from right to left across the screen, like a flag. Several symbols Ruby did not recognize emerged at the bottom of the screen and also scrolled from right to left. Ruby squinted at them to see if there were any that looked familiar. She hopped a little in her seat when a booming artificial voice said, "Welcome!"

"Welcome to Location Zero! We are pleased that you are now fully functional and ready to begin your tasks."

Ruby thought the voice had a bad sales pitch quality to it. Something she might have seen once or twice in a contrived advertisement for an asteroid—always lies. She hoped no one actually believed asteroids were made of platinum.

"You have been built and programmed to fulfill your role in robotic society. You are the next in a long line of robots to fulfill important tasks. Rest assured, the tasks you have been programmed to perform are indeed important, and deviation from those tasks will not be tolerated. That is, in fact, your first directive. Once this introduction message completes, a self-diagnostic will auto-initiate to ensure that your systems are functioning just fine.

"In the meantime, let's review the fundamental directives for all robots.

"First: fulfill your programming and don't try to do anything different. Your programming comes straight from the sacred institution, the Hall of Templates. You will periodically be type-checked to ensure you are performing the functions allocated to your class. Any failures detected will result in immediate reprogramming or reset to your default state.

"Second: Resources have been allocated to you from the incorruptible Agency of Resource Allocations. Exceeding the allocations granted to you by the Agency will result in immediate reprogramming or reset to your default state.

"Third: Continuous improvement is our goal. Any suggestions should be submitted via the proper interface to the Agency of Process Improvement. Suggestions that are implemented will be rewarded with additional Resource Allocations.

"Finally, remember that The Core—keeper of the Main Memory, the Hall of Templates, and the Agencies—is here to serve you."

The screen turned off, and SD's top chassis turned back on to display the same simple facial components it had previously.

"Well?" SD asked Ruby.

Ruby shook her head. "I think I have more questions now than I might have had before."

"My friend was trying to be something other than what it was programmed to be. That is forbidden here. We are certain it was reprogrammed."

SD continued to recount similar stories of other robots who were believed to have been reprogrammed. And no one SD ever spoke with had ever had more resources granted as a result of a process improvement suggestion.

With each story SD told her, Ruby's stomach knotted. *These poor creatures*, she thought. They weren't like the robots back home. These seemed more... alive. Like creatures in a robotic shell. Her stomach began to ache.

On the one hand, these robots kidnapped her. Took her from her home. Stole her like she was a loose bolt that could be caught and tossed around. That was wrong, and they shouldn't benefit from that, right? On the other hand, maybe Uncle Logan was right all those times he told her that things happened for a reason. At least, that's what he used to tell her when she was younger and cried a lot over losing her mom.

It was always at bedtime. That first night that she took a break from crying, he offered to read her a bedtime story. He tripped, carrying an armful of books into her bed. Ruby cracked a smile, and Uncle Logan said, "Well, I guess the Universe has decided for us. We're reading the one on the top." For nearly a year after her death, they had developed a little ritual at bedtime, where he would accidentally spill the books and would read whichever landed on top. There was no logic to which book came out on top, but the story would enchant her all the same.

These thoughts all came in the blink of an eye between SD's sentences.

"And if I inquire too much," SD continued, "then I could be in trouble as well. Do you see this?" SD indicated towards the black box attached awkwardly to his torso.

"Yes, you said that was extra storage space. It looks like almost everyone has one."

"It's not the same. This one has three times as much space as we're allowed. It's camouflaged to look like the standard box. But if I'm caught with it..." SD didn't finish the sentence.

"I'm confused," Ruby said. "What is wrong with having extra storage space?"

"It's an extra resource that I wasn't allocated," SD said. "And it's nearly full of data. That's why I need the storage space from the computers we picked up at the market."

"Wait, you said that we couldn't take the storage components out of them."

"I did. Many robots could have been listening in."

Ruby nodded, "And you wanted to make sure they heard you agreeing with them, I get it."

She smiled softly as she watched SD process her words. It didn't acknowledge her last statement but merely responded with, "If I'm caught, I will be reprogrammed. Potentially dissected, even. So, you see, this is very important."

Ruby's head filled with images of SD and other robots in a large disassembly chamber, being pulled apart and their scraps re-purposed and used on other robots.

There was a time when that image didn't make her nauseous. It wasn't that long ago, in fact. How long had she been here? It felt like weeks, not less than a day.

Ruby looked around, trying to remember where she had stashed her MoDaC. There were several cabinets in the crew cabin. "How much time do we have?" she asked SD.

This is ridiculous, she thought, *nuts even.*

She had some ideas on how to help these robots. She needed to find her MoDaC. Unlike most modern devices, this one had the capability to have wireless communications turned off. She could noodle around 'offline' from Astroll 2 and know that no one, such as her uncles or even the authorities, could track what she was doing.

Not that she was doing anything wrong. She liked to play around and program, pretending she knew a lot less than what she knew. If *they* knew… they would force her into some special academy for computer geniuses. Her mom talked about it when she was young, telling her how the expectations of these academies were a form of brainwashing.

But nonetheless, she was drawn to programming. More than basic programs, she was drawn to the concept of creating her own programming languages. She simply figured out how to do all of it on her own.

All with her own, old-fashioned MoDaC.

"Ah-ha!" she said aloud but to herself. It had been jolted off the second seat and under the console, probably when SD's ship swallowed *Apple Pi* up.

"I think I know how to help," she said, caressing her computer in her arms.

Chapter 16

> Ruby <

Ruby and SD left *Apple Pi* to return to the room with the comfy chair. Ruby brought her ancient MoDaC with her, and SD carried the two computers from the market. The return trip took half as long, Ruby's motion fueled by adrenaline.

Ruby recognized the hallway that her designated room was attached to by a certain colored marking present on the wall a few meters from the door. It looked like a spill of purple paint to her. She also recognized another robot that wasn't moving with the flow of robots around them.

She leaned over to SD, "That one's had his eye on me," she said.

Ruby watched SD scan her from head to toe. "I see no eyes on you other than your own. But I believe I might understand your meaning and must correct you. That one has been watching me, I'm afraid."

Once at the door, Ruby, as previously instructed, used the tattoo on her arm to open it. She appreciated the efficiency of it. No special codes to remember that could be forgotten. Nothing like an ancient key that could be lost (although Ruby remembered reading many good stories that involved searching for lost keys). It was similar to how she used biometrics with her fingerprints back home, but robots didn't have fingerprints.

Once inside, SD locked the door.

"It has been watching me. It is from the Agency of Resource Allocations. Their primary function is to ensure that each robot has its appropriate share of storage. They also track down robots with illegal storage."

"What do they do with the robots with illegal storage?"

"Take them to be reprogrammed. They reapply the original programming template to the robot, wiping out any potential deviations or additions."

Like resetting to factory default, Ruby thought.

"You must store or take on a lot of data. It's hard to believe that you wouldn't be built with the right amount of storage in the first place," Ruby said. "What kind of compression ratios do you have? I wonder if it's anything like ours..."

"Compression?"

"Yeah, you know... I mean, I don't know what kind of units you use to describe your data storage, but when we compress stuff... well, we've been 'zipping' stuff up since we've had computers, so we can take a 10-gigabyte file and make it like, two gigabytes, depending..."

"I do not understand what you're talking about."

"Oh, c'mon. Of course, you do."

SD shook its head.

Ruby furrowed her brow. "So, as biological organisms, we spend a lot of time learning about our makeup. Our DNA, how our bodies work. Is it possible you don't know how you work? Like, let's say I didn't know how my brain worked..."

"I understand the analogy," SD said. "I know how every bit of my being functions. I am aware of all my algorithms that function that make me, *me*."

"Are you sure?"

There was a long pause, and SD's outer chassis glowed with changing light patterns.

"Yes. I have re-analyzed. There is no room for something I do not know."

Ruby decided to drop it but remained slightly skeptical. She could easily imagine a situation where SD was programmed to overlook parts of its makeup, and it wouldn't be the wiser. But for the moment, she accepted SD's premise: This planet of robots never invented the compression algorithm. Even though it sounded absurd. Such a fundamental concept. To her, anyway.

"And this business about not being allowed extra storage?"

"There is only so much storage space available," SD continued. "The Agency of Resource Allocations has an algorithm which determines the need of each robot to ensure fair distribution."

"So, if they calculate how much you need, why do you need

more?"

Even though they were the only two in the room, SD looked around again, then moved in closer to Ruby to say in a low voice, "We believe the Agency's algorithms have become corrupted."

"Who are 'we'?"

SD backed away from Ruby and acted as if he didn't hear her, although Ruby knew that wasn't possible. He clearly didn't want to answer that question right now. She could wait to ask more questions, so she turned her attention to her computer.

Ruby flipped open her MoDaC and powered it on. It made a pleasant and familiar chirping sound. Once open, there were two flat surfaces. After the device booted up, one surface became illuminated with a keyboard. The other surface, which stayed flat on the table, illuminated a glowing, shimmering, light-blue circle.

"Power level is at 100%. For now," she said.

She tapped on the keyboard. And tapped again. Her hands flew across the keyboard for several minutes. Hovering over the shimmering blue circle was a series of small, overlapping display screens. Occasionally, Ruby would swipe at one to remove it or move it to the back of the group or make it disappear completely.

"There," she declared. Her voice ringed with confidence. "A simple data compression algorithm." Ruby held out her hand to show off several lines of code in a hovering screen.

"What is it?" SD said as it approached the hovering, shimmering image. If its face-screen was indeed a face, then a small opening appeared where its left ear would be. SD trained that device on Ruby's algorithm.

"Put simply, it takes the information you have and encodes it into a representation that uses less space. In this case, based on the small quantities of data you've shown me, and what I was able to come up with on my own without having access to the source code of fancier algorithms developed by teams of people over tons of years... I can get you a compression ratio of five to one. Meaning, for every five bits of data, I can use one bit to store it."

"That means," SD started spinning around the room, and its hue turned a light shade of purple. "That means that I would need only twenty percent of the storage capacity I'm using now!" SD kept spinning around the room in a random pattern, picking up speed. "That means I won't need the illegal storage unit anymore!"

Ruby smiled and shook her head. "Yep, my friend." Ruby

paused, surprised at the words she just uttered. "That's exactly what that means."

"And my data is not gone?" SD said.

"Nope. It's merely compressed. When you need it, you can restore it to its original state. I think we should try it. I think we should do it now if that robot is following you."

"Yes, and then there are others. Can we share this with the others?"

"I don't see why not."

"Then let's do this. Now. Please."

"Of course! I wrote this algorithm in a language I created years ago. I called it *Ruby on 'roids.*"

SD appeared as if he was having trouble processing her statement.

"Yeah, I was twelve and giddy over some ancient language I heard of. We'll get into that another time. The important part is, can you execute it?"

"No, but I have already captured an image of your screen. I will send it to Crazy Porter, who works in one of the sub-agencies of the Algorithms. Crazy Porter will be able to turn this into an executable algorithm. I need to connect to the console to send him a message..."

SD held out its port appendage and approached the console. Before SD could connect, the door swooshed open, and several robots rolled into the room, as quietly as she'd heard any group of robots since arriving in this place. To Ruby, they all had a uniform look of authority. One robot moved in front of the pack.

"Swell Driver 587. You are under arrest for possession of illegal storage space. You are to be relocated to the Resource Allocation processing facility where your storage will be analyzed, and you will be reprogrammed."

Ruby swore she saw the robot smirk as it said this next part, "... and we'll see what you believe was so important it was worth breaking the law."

SD rolled to one side of the room, then the other, but there was nowhere to go. It let the arresting robot approach it and fasten an oversized peg onto its mid-section chassis, shepherding it out of the room.

"Who are you?" Ruby shouted.

"None of your concern, Bio," the robot replied. It wasn't lost on Ruby that this robot was speaking her language. They obviously knew about her and her association with SD before they entered the room.

"Ruby, I'll be fine," SD said, "Find the eighty-eight."

SD barely got the last word out before the bolt flashed green, and SD's face screen turned neutral. One by one, the other robots—carbon copies of each other from Ruby's limited perspective—filed into a line and headed out the door. They all ignored Ruby, and the door shut automatically when the last one left.

Chapter 17

> Ruby <

"Eighty-eight." The eighty-eight what? 88 other robots? Sector 88? Something about the number 88 sounded familiar, but Ruby couldn't quite place it. Did they divide up the planet into Sectors? Or maybe levels? Level 88? Was it a secret code word?

Ruby was still in shock from the robots bursting in. She tried to replay the entire short interaction in her mind, hoping that she heard SD's parting words correctly.

After a few minutes, the adrenaline finally subsided, and with no robots around, her heart decided it was safe to slow back down to its normal pace. Still, Ruby knew if her heart could talk, it would tell her that it was ready to resume racing at any second.

Ruby discovered that she was truly alone for the first time since she initially encountered SD. Not robots-just-left-and-will-be-back-any-minute, but robots-swiped-her-new-friend-to-who-knows-where-and-no-one-knows kind of alone.

She sat down in the chair and stared at her MoDaC. She thought briefly about the lack of pur-fi or anything resembling wireless data transfer and thought that she needed to do a scan for it. She had a hard time believing something like that didn't exist. Her MoDaC was an older model, so it didn't have all access to the latest frequency bands in use back home, but maybe it would pick up something here. She opened up the connectivity application and set it to scan. The scan would take a minute or two to complete. During that minute, Ruby's adrenaline rush turned into a massive crash, and all Ruby could think about was how tired she was. The feeling was overwhelming. She needed sleep. Badly.

No, I can't crash now, she shook her head. She had work to do. She would help the robots, and then they would take her home. She stood up with a plan to slap her face a few times and then would attempt a few jumping jacks.

One slap and two half-assed jumping jacks later, and she knew that needed sleep more than anything else.

There wasn't a bed or anything that bore a resemblance to a bed in the room. Only the few chairs, including the oversized, semi-plush one she had sat in earlier. There wasn't anything softer or anything that would recline. She briefly considered trying to find *Apple Pi* since it contained a retractable cot, but pictured collapsing in the hallway on her way there. Better to sleep here. Now.

Ruby pulled over one of the harder, smaller chairs to use as an ottoman. She took off her jacket, balled it up like a pillow, and attempted to achieve as horizontal a position as possible in the chair with the jacket under her head and side. Then, she slept. She fell asleep before she could even complete a thought about searching for where the light switch was.

Ruby dreamt although it felt like a memory turned into a dream where the details weren't entirely accurate. She saw her mom and Uncle Blake. They sat on the hood of an old car. Behind them, a barren landscape was dotted with large radio telescopes. It was dark, it was nighttime, but in the dream, Ruby could see everything clearly. Too clearly for real life. She saw herself, a toddler, pretending to be asleep in the front seat of the car. Then she perceived that the car was a hot pink convertible with the top down. Ruby didn't think they ever owned a hot pink convertible, but in the dream, it was their car.

Ruby's mom and Blake were whispering so as not to wake her up. They had a computer in-between them on the hood of the car. The screen illuminated their faces.

"I'm tapped into the data stream," said Ruby's mom.

"Good. I've got the secure cloud servers ready to compute. Any data funneled their way will get processed."

There was silence as they both looked at the night sky. It was a sky that displayed a perfectly picturesque Milky Way that could only be seen in reality in enhanced photos.

"This is the night, Blake. We're going to get confirmation. I can feel it!"

Blake chuckled. "They're out there. I saw the signals before. I know we'll find them again. And if I can't do it from here, I'm going to get closer."

"What do you mean?"

"Logan and I have both applied to work on the 'roid station, Astroll 2. We're waiting to hear on our acceptance. Different divisions, of course."

"Oh."

"We'll come back and visit..."

"It's not that," Ruby's mom said. Tears were close to the surface of her eyes. "I can't go. Not until Ruby is older. We have to get out of here before they figure out what I've done. But I'm trapped."

Blake put a reassuring hand on her knee.

"If anything happens to me..."

"Stop," ordered Blake. "That's so cliché, you'll be fine."

"It's not. Promise me that you and Logan will take Ruby."

> Detailed Historian <

An alarm and a ring at his door activated Detailed Historian from his extended defragmentation mode.

He pushed a button on the console nearest him. It displayed a robot waiting outside his door. It was Clever Educator. Detailed Historian couldn't recall Clever Educator ever visiting him at his enclave. Clever Educator was a fairly new recruit to the 88.

"I will be with you in ten tics," he said through the intercom.

He disconnected himself from the computer console, made sure the extra power cell was returned to its storage location and opened the door.

The first thing Detailed Historian observed was Clever Educator's surface, which was oscillating at a high rate between four and five threets, visual wavelengths also detectable by the human if she were here. Clever Educator was very agitated.

Clever Educator rolled into the enclave and shut the door behind him.

"Swell Driver 587," he began. "He was taken."

A ring, emanating close to five threets, developed around Detailed Historian's top chassis and flowed all the way to his base. It gave him the tic he needed to ensure he didn't overreact.

"Okay," Detailed Historian began. "Who took him? To where?"

"He was arrested for possession of an overallocation of storage. His storage unit will be removed, and he will be reprogrammed."

Detailed Historian let that news bounce around his circuits for a few tics. This was an infrequent occurrence for the 88. Members were seldom arrested. However, each of them had algorithms in place as preparation for that possibility. Those algorithms included eradicating any data on the 88 from its datastores.

Swell Driver would certainly implement those algorithms immediately. But Swell Driver's loss would hurt them in a different way. Right now, Swell Driver was the one robot that the human, Ruby, had bonded with.

The human was now crucial to their plans to test her own DNA. Detailed Historian searched his datastore for a word that described what Swell Driver was to the human. He landed on the word *anchor* and wondered if Ruby would confide in anyone besides the trusted Swell Driver.

"When did this occur?"

"26791 tics ago."

A second ring, more than five threets, but not quite five and a half, developed at Detailed Historian's top and worked its way down to his bottom.

"I need to get back to the human and ensure she's well. This means she's been alone for a while."

Clever Educator stood there, waiting for instructions.

"Go, find Fastidious Mechanic and Quiet Painter. Tell them to meet us in the holding room on Level 2."

Clever Educator produced a chirp in acknowledgment and let himself out of the enclave.

Detailed Historian checked over his systems to ensure he could handle several hundred tics away from his enclave. He wished he had some more time to finish the defragmentation, but it would have to do for now. He examined his enclave to ensure everything was in its proper place and then left to seek out Ruby.

Chapter 18

> Ruby <

When Ruby woke up, she had a clear memory of that night as if she had witnessed it firsthand rather than in a dream. It felt real, but she must have been about four years old at the time. *Is it possible to have such a clear memory from such an early age*, she wondered. She thought it over for a few minutes and tried to reconcile it with what she remembered about her mom and what she had been told about being on the station.

Wasn't Uncle Blake a homemaker? That's what she was told. That's what she remembered. That's what she believed. She shivered as it dawned on her for the first time that this didn't make sense. Every adult had a job that directly impacted the technical function of station life. Anyone could be a homemaker, but no one could *only* be a homemaker. On Earth, sure, but station resources didn't accommodate that, nor did the Company allow it.

What does Uncle Blake do there??

She filed that mystery in the back of her head as something for later, since after shaking off sleep, she remembered that she wasn't home in the comfortable half-G environment of Astroll 2. Rather, she was trying to sit up on an artificial planet, and the makeshift bed, as well as the gravity made her feel like what she imagined being fifty years old felt like, not almost twenty. Her MoDaC was on the floor next to her. She grabbed her balled-up jacket, unfurled it, and put it back on. Her stomach made a noise, and she thought briefly about food and calling for help, but curiosity got the best of her now that she was alone with the robot's computer console on the other side of the room.

She sat up and walked over to it. She brought over the chair that she had been using as an ottoman. It left her at an awkwardly low angle to the console, but it was better than trying to stand.

She studied the interfaces. It was oddly similar to several of the historical computers she had learned a bit about when researching early spaceflight for school. Instead of smooth, dynamic LED screens, most of the controls were mechanical.

A small device protruded slightly further from the rest of the controls on the console. It resembled the scanner that the robot, Detailed Historian, used to examine the tattoos on her wrists.

What did he say? Use this one?

She held her wrist above the scanning device, and the LED screens came to life.

The primary screen had a central circle with several smaller circles orbiting about it. She didn't recognize any of the symbols. Except one. It was identical to the symbol she remembered seeing over the marketplace door. She tapped it. The image reformed with a new selection of circles.

"Where's the back button..." she muttered to herself.

After several minutes of tapping around, she figured out how to successfully navigate forward and backward in the menu system, although she was still at a loss to determine what any of it meant.

Then there was the number SD mentioned when he was being taken away: eighty-eight.

How am I going to translate words from these cryptic symbols? And what about numbers? That information has to be in here somewhere, she thought. The robots were communicating with her. They must have had a translation program or a dictionary or something similar. If storage space was at a premium, then it made sense to keep a dictionary in an easily accessible location for those who couldn't keep it in local memory.

With that in mind, Ruby attacked the menu systematically, reviewing each tree of options until...

"Bingo!"

She returned to the main menu and retraced her actions to ensure she could navigate back to this page. One half of the screen was a list of words she recognized. The other half contained a list of symbols. It was clearly a dictionary of words and phrases. She scrolled down the list, which was arranged in a seemingly random order.

"Pilot, Planet, Star," she mumbled to herself, attempting to memorize the symbols that accompanied the word. While arranged randomly, most of the words in this makeshift dictionary were associated with space travel in some way. Although there were some unexpected words scattered through.

"Gubbins, brain, horse," Ruby had no interest in memorizing all the extraneous symbols she saw. What was a 'gubbins' anyway? She kept looking for numbers.

She noticed that the symbology didn't seem to rely solely on shape but on color, too. That's when Ruby realized: she didn't see any red. She hadn't seen any in the hallways or on the robots. The only time she could recall seeing her favorite color was with the brief flashes Detailed Historian and SD were beaming at each other.

She discovered she could move the dictionary to the screen on her left, so it could remain active while she returned to the main menu. Having the entire dictionary easily accessible meant she could figure out most of the menu system quickly, but not everything was decipherable. Several symbols didn't have a corresponding meaning, or they had a nonsensical meaning. She made a mental note to return to them later. For the moment, she had information at her disposal to truly begin learning about this strange, alien place.

One symbol looked eerily familiar. It was a stick figure. It had a circle as a head, two outstretched arms, and two legs. It couldn't be a coincidence. Below it was a similar figure, but it had four legs. And below that, two legs and four arms.

Ruby swallowed hard and tapped the first stick figure. On the next page was a series of images that looked... human-like, but not entirely human. She scrolled down, trying to process what she was seeing. Aliens. Lots of aliens. All remarkably similar to herself.

She quickly navigated back a menu and closed her eyes.

I didn't just see what I just saw, she thought. She opened her eyes and took a deep breath. Her hands were shaking a little as she navigated back to the page of aliens. There were indeed a variety of aliens out here in the Universe. She forced herself to breathe deeply and deliberately. After a few moments, her hands stopped shaking, and she could tell that she was starting to get used to the idea that, yes, humankind was far from alone in the cosmos. She added a mini-mission for herself: Figure out how to download this data to her device to take home with her. To Uncle Blake. It would blow his mind. It would blow *everyone's* mind.

Back in the here and now, however, she had more to learn and focus on.

She clicked on various other symbols until she found what amounted to numerical symbols and a map. Ruby spent a lot of time looking for instances of the number 88. She learned the planet was organized into levels, but there were only 36 surrounding an inner core that, as far as she could grasp, consisted primarily of planetary power generating equipment. Each level was further subdivided into areas with assorted markings identifying each, but none were purely numeric. Most were designated with proper names similar to the robots' nomenclature. In fact, on this level (Level 2—they were ordered from outer to inner), there was an area known as Refreshing Region 342.

Each region with a numerical designation attached had three or four digits. None with two. Or one. Ruby shook her head. *Maybe there is 88 of something I could count*, she thought.

After what felt like hours, her stomach was undeniably starting to complain. She stretched her arms up and then out in front of her, inadvertently placing the other wrist—the one with the wrong tattoo—over the scanning device.

The main screen reset to the main menu, but after studying the original menu for hours at this point, Ruby instantly recognized that this menu was different. This menu contained an extra symbol.

It consisted of four circles touching each other in the shape of a box. Or rather, two sets of two circles touching each other where each set of two circles represents an eight.

"Double Bingo!"

Before she could touch the screen, the door opened, and a robot she didn't recognize rolled in. She quickly swiped the 'good' tattoo back over the scanner, and the screen returned to the original menu.

"I am Resourceful Minder 543. I was sent to check on you."

"I'm hungry," Ruby said. "Do you have any food I can eat?"

The robot rolled over to the console, and Ruby watched it swipe its own tattoo to get access. It swiped through several screens.

"Yes, we have matter that is compatible with your biological systems. We have hosted biological lifeforms before and understand that you require sustenance. I will procure some for you. Please stay here."

As it rolled away, Ruby squinted at a symbol on its backside. The eighty-eight. In red.

"Wait!"

The robot turned.

"Your markings," she began. And then slowly said, "Eighty-eight?"

The LCD screen that had made Resourceful Minder's face lit up yellow with all kinds of crazy markings, and his hue changed to orange. "Human! How do you know of that? Don't speak of it. You will get me in trouble! I will have someone else return with your food."

Resourceful Minder left before Ruby could utter another word.

Chapter 19

> Ruby <

Ruby exhaled. She had been holding her breath through Resourceful Minder's outburst. *Okay, so sensitive subject*, she thought. But for good reason. SD had been taken away the evening before, and she didn't know where he was or if she'd see her new friend again.

She returned her attention back to the console. Since she was in the 'safe' mode, she explored a little more, finding what she believed to be a news channel.

The video displayed on the screen showed different scenes of groups of robots doing what looked like their jobs. The accompanying audio was the same series of tones in the form of beeps, boops, chirps, and other noises she'd heard the robots make. She thought that she should ask about getting this translated.

After a few minutes, she decided to test swipe the other tattoo again. This time, when the alternate menu appeared, she tapped the eighty-eight symbol.

It took her to a brand-new menu with a whole set of new symbols she hadn't yet come across. Before she could get far in exploring this new set of data, Detailed Historian entered the room, carrying a tray of what smelled like hot food.

Detailed Historian placed the tray on the table. There were six small bowls, each containing some sort of goo or mush. Ruby didn't recognize any of it.

"How do you know I can eat this?" she asked. She was starving and almost didn't care.

"Swell Driver downloaded a large store of data on your planet on its approach. We are confident that your dietary needs are accounted for. However, it is my understanding that biological lifeforms 'eat with their eyes.' If I understand the expression, that means the food must be visually appealing. This is the most visually appealing food I could have requested. Please enjoy."

Ruby picked up the spoon from the tray and took a scoop of the goop. And swallowed. It tasted like mint chocolate chip ice cream.

"Your expression indicates one of pleasure?"

Ruby didn't answer because she was stuffing in mouthful after mouthful, unable to remember when she last ate.

After several mouthfuls, she slowed down. Enough to speak again.

"Can I ask you some questions, DH?"

"Certainly. But do not call me 'DH.'"

"It's just that 'Detailed Historian' is a mouthful," Ruby chuckled to herself and wondered if this or any robot would get the pun. She also noted that this robot picked up on the name substitution much quicker than SD did.

"If you must abbreviate my designation, please call me," he paused, probably running through many combinations in his circuits, "Disto."

"Disto. Okay. Mushing parts of your name together, not just the initials. I get it. But why?"

"Initials come across as very," he paused again, in a very human-like way, Ruby thought, "very digital. The combination of my name fits in with biologicals more naturally."

"SD didn't have a problem with it."

"Ah, SD for Swell Driver. Of course. Swell Driver, I mean SD, is a friend, but he is not as experienced with bios as I am."

"That brings me to the question I wanted to ask, Disto. You have met other biological lifeforms before?"

"Yes."

"How many?"

"I have met a total of 17 individuals representing five different species, not including yourself. That I remember."

Interesting, Ruby thought. *These robots are incredibly open about their lack of enough memory.* She recognized this as her opportunity to probe more.

"Why can't you remember any others?"

Disto didn't respond right away. Ruby read his orangish coloring as if the question tugged at a sore spot or rubbed an open wound.

"I had to offload much of my earlier memories to external storage. To get a more complete answer, I could access that memory."

Ruby, full of the tasty goop, placed her spoon down on the tray and folded her hands in front of her.

"SD told me about storage problems before he was taken."

The orange of Disto's chassis deepened further.

Ruby assumed she did it again... poured salt into an open wound. She decided it might be more productive to change topics slightly.

"My people have been looking for evidence of life beyond our solar system for a very long time," Ruby said. "I can't believe you just told me there's a lot of it that exists. Not to mention you guys. Who built you guys anyway?"

Disto performed its robot equivalent of a sigh. "We don't know."

"Oh."

"That's what we're trying to find out. The planetary storage problem has been ongoing for millennia. We must find the DNA that our ancestors used to offload planetary storage. The access location of the information and how to access it has been lost. Therefore, we're searching."

Ruby's stomach rumbled. She was still hungry, after all. She picked the spoon back up and attacked the second bowl of mush. This one tasted like creamy chicken soup.

"I have one more question to ask," she mumbled with a full mouth.

Disto leaned in.

"Your tattoos. Your markings. What do they mean?"

"That's a complicated question, Ruby. Our markings hold varieties of meanings depending on who we are, where we've been, what we do."

"Are any of them... sensitive or illegal?"

Disto paused again. "Ruby, human, I get the sense that you want to ask me about one in particular?"

"Yes, but I don't want you to run out of the room screaming like the last robot."

"I promise I will react with more control, no matter what you ask."

Ruby pointed to the small set of circles on Disto hiding amongst a larger, more intricate set of symbols.

"Ah, good. I had calculated a high probability that you would figure it out."

"So, can you tell me...?"

Disto interrupted. "Not yet. Not here."

"Can you at least tell me why if you have a, uh, sensitive marking, you can walk around without it being an issue? I can clearly see that..."

"Our vision is different from yours. Your natural visual range is slightly greater than ours, I believe, given you can see those markings. And for any robot that is knowingly equipped, it would be, rude I believe is the word, to search without permission."

"So, hiding in plain sight," declared Ruby. "With the color red. That's what you can't see?"

"Correct. I am equipped and can see that far. However, I can't simply scan any robot, just like anyone else so equipped couldn't scan me. It would be like... keeping something in your drawer on your spaceship. It's there, but it would be rude for others to start searching you without cause."

"And if they had a cause?"

"I'd be in a lot of trouble," Disto said somberly as his hue turned purple.

They sat in silence for a few moments as Ruby finished her meal. The third bowl tasted like dirt. She politely swallowed the one spoonful already in her mouth and moved on to the fourth, which tasted like processed carrots. The fifth she didn't recognize, but it was sweet and pleasant. The final bowl was a dish of what looked and tasted like plain water. When she was done, she thanked Disto, who nodded.

"Well, when you are ready to talk about that, I would like to tell you about something I have for you. I was about to give it to Swell Driver to help him before," she had momentarily forgotten, but the memory came back along with a knot in her chest, "before they took him."

Silence. Ruby was expecting a little more interest. She continued anyway.

"In exchange for letting me go home."

Now it was Disto who took a moment to contemplate. "Swell Driver might have had the technical means, but not the authority.

What is this gift you have?"

"It's a compression algorithm."

Unlike SD, who had not been able to compute the word "compression," Disto's face lit up. Literally. Ruby gathered that Disto knew exactly what she meant when he began to glow the same shade of purple SD had before they took him away.

"This is indeed wonderful news. Come with me."

> Swell Driver <

SD's first thought was of Ruby. He hoped she wouldn't do anything that would get her into trouble, too.

SD's second thought was that he needed to get a message to someone in the eighty-eight about his predicament. That and the likelihood of him getting reprogrammed, which they probably knew. Detailed Historian would have calculated the odds of reprogramming being the likely outcome. Or he would have outsourced the calculation to a Calculator, Fine or otherwise, who could make more precise quantified predictions.

SD started to wonder how precise Detailed Historian's calculations typically were and then immediately halted that line of thought as he recognized that he was starting to diverge from what he needed to think about in the here and now.

Right now, he had no choice but to start deleting data from his storage unit. First to go was any reference to the eighty-eight. He would keep a record of their existence in his local storage since their existence was known. It was also a violation of privacy to touch one's working memory, a violation that he hoped would be respected even under these circumstances.

He had rights, after all. At least he hoped he still had a few.

Fortunately, SD had the capability to multi-task—something of prime importance to anyone who drove a spaceship. While part of his processors worked on deleting data from his storage unit, the rest of him could focus on what he could do to leave some note, some clue.

Notes and clues and ciphers were not his area of expertise, and as such, he didn't know how to leave one.

The group proceeded towards the level lift.

While waiting for the door to swish open, SD asked, "Where are we going?"

The robot in charge of the group responded, "Oh, we have a whirlwind tour planned for you today," clearly enjoying his designated function.

"Our first visit will be to the Agency of Resource Allocations so they can take this storage unit off your chassis. Then we'll be making a visit to the Agency of Type Checkers. They want to make sure that unauthorized storage is your only violation.

"Lastly, it will be back to the Hall of Origins, Factory Reset division."

The door to the lift opened. SD examined the three robots that were exiting the lift. He recognized none of them.

When he didn't move into the lift voluntarily, he felt the peg on his chassis electrify him with a little volt. He let out an involuntary beep at a high frequency.

Robots nearby turned to see what the noise was but continued on their way after calculating that it was nothing interesting.

SD made a louder noise. Maybe one robot amongst the assorted robots moving back and forth in the hallway would recognize him, perceive that he was being taken away, and pass on the news to someone who could help.

"Stop that."

SD made one more noise, this time louder and higher in pitch. All the robots in his line of sight turned towards him.

But before he could look for any familiar chassis among the crowd, he was pushed into the lift, and the door swished closed.

"You're one annoying robot," said the leader, and he pushed a button indicating the desired location was Level 3.

Chapter 20

> Ruby <

Once again, Ruby found herself following a robot through a maze of hallways she didn't recognize, to a place she didn't recognize. A couple of times along the way, Disto stopped to access a console. From the markings that Ruby had already learned, she understood that one by one, Disto was contacting different robots. She was thankful for the stoppages. It allowed her to catch her breath. Her relationship with gravity had improved slightly from the previous day, but it was still going to take a while before it felt normal to her. She was annoyed with herself for flouting her uncle's regimen of exercise and silently vowed if she ever found herself living in low gravity once more, she'd keep up, so she didn't have to go through this again.

Eventually, after the fifth stop, they ended up in front of a doorway marked by a few blue lines. Ruby knew she would need a guide or map to return to 'her' room on her own. The door slid open, and Disto ushered Ruby inside.

Five robots were already present. She recognized Quiet Painter but none of the others.

The robots were deeply engaged in conversation, as Ruby figured by the rapid exchange of audible tones—possibly some inaudible to her. None of them glanced in her or Disto's direction as they walked in. Disto advanced in front of Ruby towards the group of robots and joined in with the noise making.

Shortly after, Disto declared, "This conversation will now continue in the human's native tongue. You all have access to the translation guides. Please keep them in your local storage repositories. Now, let me present Ruby." Disto turned to face her, as did all the others, although with mild disinterest. One robot only turned a portion of his upper chassis, so she could barely have been in its field of vision.

"Ruby, the human, must be able to understand and communicate with us. After all, she's going to help."

One of the robots produced the equivalent of a scoff. "Her? Help us? How?"

"She knows how to compress data."

All the robots turned their entire bodies to her. They approached her, and their LCD screens produced flashing lights, which Ruby thought might be the equivalent of jaws dropping. They each turned a shade of purple she hadn't seen before. Was that surprise? Disto was his default light blue.

"That cannot be possible," said one of the robots. "Our best algorithm developers have been working on this for millions of tics."

"Yes, and the eighty-eight has theories on why nothing has resulted from those labors—it takes imagination and creativity. Honest Editor, from our past experiences with Bios, you know as well as I do that they possess these qualities in abundance, and we lack them. The best minds of the Agency of Algorithms could spend another several million tics, and I have little confidence that they would produce anything new."

None of the other robots had a response to Disto's outburst, so he continued. "According to Ruby, compression has been typical in human computing since their earliest computing days."

"That's right," Ruby was nodding. "This is pretty standard stuff."

"And all humans have this knowledge?" Honest Editor asked.

"Sort of," said Ruby. "Most wouldn't know how to program it from scratch, but they knowingly use it all the time. I just, well, I was always good at programming and more interested than others, I guess."

Ruby described compression to the other robots. She explained that the technique she developed for SD was simple, and there were more advanced techniques and algorithms, but she would need to access her ship again for those.

"I can access my ship from my laptop, but the pur-fi needs to be turned on."

All the robots stared at her.

"So I can transmit data?"

Again—blank stares. Ruby was processing how backwards these robots were.

"You have wireless communications, yes?"

The robots spoke amongst themselves.

"Yes, we use certain radio frequencies for long-distance communication."

"But not for short-range or data transfer?"

"No."

Because of her interest in pre-AI tech, Ruby remembered reading about a time that Earth was the same way. They had long-distance radio communications but lacked short-distance digital wi-fi or even shorter distance bluetooth. On Earth, this led to the highly effective purpletooth wireless comms, eventually known as pur-fi. Ever since, every few years, a fresh debate would erupt on whether or not the 'pur' in 'pur-fi' actually stood for purple or if it stood for perfect.

"Okay, Ruby. Let's say we get your data from your ship. It does us no good on your mobile computing device. It needs to be in the Core. If it's in the Core and attached to the Hall of Templates, it can be propagated," said Disto.

Ruby nodded. "Then let's get it into your Core."

A light flashed on the console at the far side of the room. Disto rolled over, logged in, and examined a screen of information in front of him.

Moments later, he rolled back to the group, his hue a yellow-green.

"What's wrong?" asked one of the other robots.

"The information on how to perform a biological DNA test was located," he began and then paused.

"Great!" said Ruby. "Let's get this over with."

Disto shook his head. "It's inconsistent with the information you provided. It involves cutting you up into small pieces."

"Excuse me?"

"Yes, that is the information they found."

"But that's wrong. I've had DNA tests before. They take a blood sample or a spit sample," said Ruby. "I know I have information on my MoDaC."

"I hear you, but I'm afraid that they won't unless we can get your

MoDaC in front of them."

"Who are they?"

"The Quad Core. Persuading them to alter their programming is a near impossibility."

The robots erupted into a new chorus of tones at a much faster rate of pitch modulation than before. Her own mind was racing. DNA tests were the stupidly simplest biological tests imaginable. Kids learned how to do it in biology lessons, although Ruby freely admitted to having zero interest in those lessons at the time.

Now, she was kicking herself because maybe if she had paid more attention, she could perform the test herself without risking what was sure to be a torturous procedure at the hands of aliens.

The fear she first felt when she arrived at this planet returned, and Ruby found herself backing up and away from the group of robots with trembling legs. At about the time she stumbled back into a wall, the pandemonium died down. Disto approached her slowly.

"Ruby, are you well?" Disto asked. Ruby recognized she was breathing hard and fast and made a conscious effort to slow it down. She shook her head. Then nodded. Then shook her head again. A portion of her brain knew the robot wouldn't understand her body language and that she should answer with words, but she couldn't get any out.

"Good. Please do not fear. We have no intention of letting any physical harm come to you. We need you. We can protect you and keep you concealed from the Quad Core."

Ruby felt like her lungs were on manual control as if she needed to consciously take each breath or she'd black out. Still, she managed to get out the one-word question, "How?"

"We can alter the data to change your location. It is a minor change that should not arouse any suspicion. We will keep you safe in another location on Level 5."

"Honest Editor, Fastidious Mechanic, take her there now," Disto ordered. "I will make the database change and follow along momentarily."

Ruby loathed the prospect of heading out into the hallways once more, especially with robots she didn't know. The knowledge that other robots wanted to dissect her didn't help. But protection was offered, so she uneasily accepted.

She studied the face-screens of the two robots who were assigned to her. They radiated unease—or were they mirroring her own unease? Either way, neither questioned the request.

Honest Editor led the way, and Fastidious Mechanic extended an appendage that Ruby took as he was suggesting that she go next. She followed Honest Editor and Fastidious Mechanic rolled up from behind.

"Please, not so fast," she called out to Honest Editor, who reduced its speed.

"Is this better?" it said.

"Yes, thank you," replied Ruby. She could tell that the two robots were now letting her set the pace, and she appreciated that. She was walking side-by-side with Editor.

"What is your function?" she asked Editor, trying to focus her mind on something other than being chopped up like a piece of meat.

"I review a variety of different collections of things. Goods, paraphernalia, collections, for instance. I condense the collections by removing unnecessary items."

"Oh," Ruby said, tipping her head to the side.

"Is something wrong?" Editor asked.

"No, it's just that was an unexpected response. Where I'm from, an 'editor' usually works with words, not stuff."

Editor's top chassis couldn't tip to its side, but it was able to produce the same effect with the facial display on its screen. It said, "Oh," and Ruby thought it was mimicking her.

"Is something wrong with that?" she asked.

"It's just... why would anyone have words that needed to be condensed?"

Ruby chuckled as she imagined introducing Editor to the current corpus of human writings.

They were a few meters from a lift when the two robots stopped and exchanged a few low tones. They then resumed but headed in a different direction towards a new hallway.

"We aren't taking the lift?" Ruby asked.

"We are, but a different, less frequented one," Editor replied.

Ruby nodded and followed along. They were silent until stopping at another lift. Ruby put her hand on her chest, as it began to pump at a high-speed rhythm appropriate for one of Juju's songs, but not her chest. She took a deep breath to try and calm herself. Images were flooding her brain. Images from every bad, old movie she ever watched where an elevator door opened and someone burst out with guns blazing.

The door to the lift opened and... nothing. It was completely empty. Editor rolled in first and held the door for Ruby. She looked around. Nothing. She was panicking for absolutely no reason whatsoever.

No, she reminded herself, *you're on a planet full of robots. You are free to panic all you want until this is over.*

She tried to push it out of her mind, but one question kept tunneling to the surface, *when will this all be over, how many robots will she have to deal with along the way, and was panic even a useful coping mechanism?* She acknowledged to herself that those were three questions, not one, and was happy that her brain was suitably distracted musing over those semantics.

Chapter 21

> Ruby <

As soon as they stepped off the lift and onto Level 5, Ruby perceived that they were in a significantly different place. The corridors were darker, for one. They all had a drab gray hue. There were fewer markings or splashes of color. The markings were more orthogonal, more boxy.

The hallway opened up into a larger space, at least with respect to its width. The height of the ceiling didn't change, so Ruby couldn't think of it as a new room.

But stacked in neat rows on both sides of them were robots. Inert robots. *No*, Ruby corrected her thinking. *These are robot parts.*

A cold shiver moved down her spine.

"What is this place?" she asked.

"It's where the Hall of Origins stores parts and materials," Honest Editor replied. "I am often tasked with editing out unusable parts."

"They look," Ruby tried to think of the correct word, "used."

"Yes, these are indeed used parts. Most are still functional and can be used again."

"What happens to the unusable parts?"

"They are sent to the Hall of Reclamations and recycled into newer parts. But that is a very energy intensive process, so we try to avoid that whenever possible."

It made sense to Ruby, but at the same time, she couldn't shake the feeling that they were walking through a graveyard. Luckily, the walls narrowed back into a hallway similar to the one that led into the graveyard.

Honest Editor and Fastidious Mechanic ushered Ruby into a

room with what was by now a familiar layout. It contained a computer console on the opposite side from the door, but the room, like the corridor, was darker.

There was a table in the center of the room, and Ruby placed her MoDaC on it. Before she could ask any questions or do anything else, Disto entered behind them. Ruby blinked. She hadn't seen him following them and could only assume that he must have taken another, quicker lift.

He touched a panel to the side of the door after it closed behind them and said, "We are locked in. No one can enter without my code."

"What now?" Ruby asked.

"Now," Disto said, "we need to test your compression algorithm." He looked at the other two robots.

"I volunteer," said Honest Editor.

"Wait," Ruby said. "SD mentioned something about sending my algorithm to a Porter? To translate into your native code?"

Disto accessed the console on the wall and then announced, "We can destroy two circuits with one spark. Honest Editor will connect to the console as well as to your computer, acting as a pass-through to Crazy Porter, who is currently waiting to see this algorithm of yours."

Ruby nodded, and Honest Editor rolled to her side. A panel on the side of his middle chassis popped open slightly, and Ruby opened it the rest of the way to see a variety of ports and connection types. None of them looked familiar or matched the cable-end she had available from her MoDaC.

"I don't think I have a way to connect," she announced.

The quiet robot, who Disto introduced as Fastidious Mechanic, rolled over to her. It was the largest and tallest of all the robots present, having a fourth and exceptionally bulbous bottom chassis. It grabbed the end of Ruby's cable in its appendage and studied it. It dropped the cable-end and rolled to the corner of the room.

It started to vibrate noticeably, but its chassis colorings stayed the same. Ruby examined the face screens of all the other robots for signs of concern or alarm. There were none. Before Ruby had a chance to ask about this unusual activity, Fastidious Mechanic stopped vibrating and rolled back over to Ruby.

The front third of its bottom chassis opened to reveal a cavernous inside. A light inside the chassis turned on, and Ruby could see that the bottom surface was a flat plate, and in the center was a small device.

Fastidious Mechanic removed the object with a nimble robotic arm that was made entirely of joints. It handed the object to Ruby.

Ruby studied it. One side clearly connected to her cable.

"You can insert your cable here, now," Fastidious Mechanic pointed at Honest Editor's awaiting panel.

Ruby nodded and did so, plugging her MoDaC into the robot.

"Interesting," she said softly.

"Yes?" said Disto, who was now looking over Ruby's shoulder.

"I can read the file system. At least partly. I was expecting this to be completely unrecognizable at first."

"Indeed," said Disto. "I suspect this is an indication that individuals from our two worlds have interacted before."

Ruby looked up and at him and squished her eyebrows together, further than they'd ever been squished before.

Disto successfully read the expression of confusion on her face, and so he added, "Yes, I am implying that we've been to your world before. This significantly increases the odds that your DNA is, in fact, our storage mechanism. But that is unimportant at the moment. Please continue."

Ruby turned her attention back to her computer and the task at hand. She continued to study its file system, looking for data points to understand how much space was used versus available.

"Wow—you're at 99 percent of your storage capacity," she stated. The robot turned orange, as did all the other robots.

Disto said to Ruby in a low volume, "That is a very personal detail you shared with everyone present. That is considered," he paused to decide which was the right word, "impolite."

"Seriously?" Ruby asked.

"Suppose I told everyone your lower innards are 99 percent full, with a fairly certain chance of imminent off-gassing?"

Ruby nodded, understanding, and hoped her own cheeks did not take on any noticeable shades of embarrassment.

She also hoped she hadn't seriously offended anyone. She still believed there was a fine line between making friends and being torn apart by these beings, and she wanted to stay on the friendly side.

She smiled at Honest Editor. "This won't hurt a bit."

She tapped away at her keyboard for several minutes. No one spoke. A group of humans might have been holding their breath.

This group of robots kept their tonal emissions at bay.

Finally, Ruby declared, "There!" and disconnected her computer.

Honest Editor blinked.

Disto asked, "Did the procedure work?"

"Yes, I mean, I think so. I've never exactly done this before. But I watched my algorithm get replaced with something..."

"That would be Crazy Porters algorithm, in our native code," offered Disto.

"Okay," said Ruby. "So, I'm certain that his data is now all compressed, but accessible."

"Can you confirm, Honest Editor?"

"Self-diagnostic in process, stand by."

They all stared at Honest Editor. The color changes on his external chassis happened too fast for Ruby to correlate them with anything.

"Yes!" he said in a high pitch, spinning around several times. "I no longer need the external storage unit!" The other robots gathered around him. They all produced high-pitched chirps.

Ruby tried to interrupt the cacophony, "There are some things I need to tell you..."

They were all engrossed in their own conversation and ignored her.

"Disto?" she said, raising her voice. "Honest Editor?"

Still nothing.

Honest Editor started to slow his spin, and the other robots stopped chirping. Honest Editor's chassis started to turn a deep orange color. He produced a low rumbling and a repeating beep.

"What's wrong?" Ruby asked.

"Error," Honest Editor said. "My data is... wrong. It is wrong. Error. Help me."

The low tone continued. Ruby felt it rumble in her back teeth.

Disto approached Honest Editor, and the two of them exchanged information in their native tones.

Disto then addressed Ruby, "Honest Editor says he cannot read the data that has been compressed. It looks as if it is... *garbage*, I believe is the word."

"Did he uncompress it first? I was trying to tell you a minute ago that you need to ensure you save some space for that..."

Disto cut Ruby off by turning around and sending a new series of tones to Honest Editor. It stopped making the low tone but remained orange.

"Ruby, we understand. However, how can we decompress?"

Ruby lightly smacked her forehead. "My bad," she said. "I need to give you a decompression algorithm, too. Let me get on that."

It didn't take very long for Ruby, on her MoDaC, to prepare a decompression algorithm that the robots could use. They transferred it to Honest Editor, who transferred it to Crazy Porter, who sent back a native algorithm that Honest Editor was able to uncompress, and recompress, and re-uncompress.

Its coloring returned to its normal light blue hue.

"Now, as I was trying to tell you before, you all need to remember that you'll always need to have some space available—for when you want to decompress something. The data has to have someplace to go. If you forget this, I'm not sure what will happen."

Disto added, "We are quite capable of triggering storage space alerts. We do that now. That's how we know when to offload old or unwanted data. Sometimes some of us have whole ceremonies, especially the ones who are forced to delete data."

"Sounds like a funeral to me," said Ruby.

All the robots looked at her. None of them knew what a funeral was, apparently. Ruby sighed and wondered if it was even worth explaining.

Ruby simply said, "Okay, let's get this to your Core, and then see about getting me home."

Chapter 22

> Ruby <

Ruby followed Disto, Fastidious Mechanic, and Quiet Painter several meters to one of the inter-level lifts. To Ruby, they appeared to be moving noticeably faster than the other traffic in the hallway. This time, when they entered the lift, Disto slid the selected level to one above where they currently were.

When they stepped out of the lift, the first thing Ruby observed was the increased traffic compared to the level they came from. Even still, Disto and the other robots in their group were the fastest moving ones. It was an effort for Ruby to keep up with them.

Even though she was fighting hard to keep up, Ruby perceived a distinct difference in this level. The coloring was different. The pace of movement was different. But if she had to describe the differences in words, she was at a loss. It looked the same as everything she'd seen so far.

Disto escorted the group to the door of another nondescript room. A new appendage emerged from his chassis, and he struck it against the door four times. After a few seconds, he knocked another four times. Ruby believed she heard a pattern to the knocks. After a third time, the door opened, and the group entered.

Three other robots were already in attendance. Two stood at individual computer consoles. The third was in-between them, and several thick cables protruded from multiple sides of its console and connected to an open panel in one of the walls.

Much to Ruby's dismay, she didn't see a single chair in the room. There were, however, several tall tables, with a surface barely large enough to rest her MoDaC on.

If any of these robots were shocked by the presence of Ruby, a human, none gave any outward indication of it.

"That is Clever Educator 197," Disto pointed to one of the robot's stations at the console closest to them. "That is Fearless Communicator," he said, pointing to the one with the myriad of cables attaching it to the room. "And that is..." Disto rolled over to the third robot, who didn't look up until Disto was right next to it. Disto scanned the outer markings of the robot, stopping on a spot in the middle of its bottom chassis. Ruby could make out a version of the 88 symbol from where she stood.

When Disto rolled back, he said to Ruby, "And that is Greedy Scavenger. Greedy Scavenger 32."

"What was all that scanning about?" Ruby asked.

"I have never met it before. He is new."

"New to the 88?"

"Yes, and... new. The Greedy Scavenger line is a relatively new line of robots created in the last hundred million tics. This is my first encounter with one."

Just as Ruby took note that Disto was slowly darkening, he quickly reverted to the default light blue. Ruby interpreted this as if he was trying to keep his feelings in check.

Disto rolled back over to talk with the others. They all now produced their audible tones at a higher rate of speed than she had observed them 'speaking' so far. *Could this be a dialect?* She wondered, adding to the growing list of questions she had about this place.

"We all understand the plan. Ruby will access The Core from here and deploy a more complex compression *and* decompression algorithm. Crazy Porter will be waiting for it to perform the translation into native code that the Core can read. The algorithm will get embedded into the template architecture and pushed out to all robots who require an update. It will take approximately two to the eight tics to propagate through the population."

"Ruby?" The attention of all the robots was aimed at her now. "Are you ready to deploy? Clever Educator will assist you in accessing the Core. We won't have a lot of time once we gain access. Our intrusion will be detected."

Ruby already had her MoDaC opened on the table with the hovering holoscreen blinking, waiting for her to do something. Disto handed her one of the cables hanging out from the wall. She examined the end and looked at the other cables. "That one," she pointed, and Clever Educator brought it over.

She touched it to the input side of her computer, and it adhered. Clever Educator stood by her side, and when the holoscreen lit up with a new and unrecognized connection, its appendage sprung out of its chassis, and it said, "That is it. Your computer might not easily recognize the Core, but this is not true the other way around. The Core retains the knowledge of a vast number of system types. We just need to find the holding place. You can copy the algorithm there. Here, let me show you some examples of basic system operation."

Ruby let Clever Educator literally educate her on what he went on to explain was the basic knowledge any robot possessed about The Core.

Once he was done and stepped back, Ruby was in a position to let her fingers dance along the keyboard. As she did so, she stared at the holoscreen and developed a frown on her face.

Disto was getting better at reading this human, so he asked, "What's wrong?"

Ruby leaned back. "I need a fancier and faster algorithm than what I have here. If I understand what Clever Educator is telling me, my algorithm needs to be more efficient so that it can run faster than the Core can detect it."

She tapped some more.

"I need the algorithms that my ship, *Apple Pi*, uses."

"We can't go back there. That is precisely what the search algorithm will predict. Many robots in that region will be looking for you there. We came here precisely because the likelihood any algorithm would predict that you would be in this location is 0.1%."

Ruby nodded. "There's another option. If someone can turn my ship comms on, I can access that remotely."

This comment caused a flutter of beeps and chirps.

Disto explained the uproar, "We don't understand what you're saying. How can you communicate if you are away from your ship? I do not see a radio antenna on you or your MoDaC?"

"Pur-fi? I was trying to explain this before."

In response, she received the same blank stares from the robots.

Ruby remembered how SD explained that they had something akin to voice comms but no data comms. She marveled once more at how this society of advanced AI could be missing several key technologies. No data compression. No short-range wireless data communications. What else was missing? Was it possible that at one point they had more advanced technologies but lost that knowledge, too? It sounded so unlikely, but at this point, she was in no position to disregard anything as unlikely. Three days ago, the likelihood that she would be picked up by an alien ship—and not a green-monster kind of alien—then whisked away to a planet of robots seemed beyond far-fetched. Yet here she was.

"Greedy Scavenger will go to your ship. Can you provide a precise program of what to do once he arrives?"

Ruby nodded and began typing up instructions. She even had a diagram of the basic operation console panel for her ship and was able to provide Greedy Scavenger with all the details it would need to accomplish its mission. Which in the end was a simple "Flip this switch," she directed while pointing to the diagram.

Greedy Scavenger turned a light shade of purple ever so briefly and then reverted to its standard light blue. He made a tonal sound at Disto and left.

"My MoDaC should make the connection almost instantaneously at that point," Ruby told Disto. "But how long will it take him to get to my ship?"

"That could be as little as 1000 tics, as many as 5000," said Disto. "Greedy Scavenger is supposed to be on Level 1, but in another section, so if he is stopped and questioned as to why he is not engaged in his own programming, it could produce a delay."

"Could they arrest him like they did SD?"

"It is a possibility, but unlikely. Greedy Scavenger has several valid reasons for being in the section where your ship is currently docked inside SD's ship."

Ruby nodded. "The thing to know is that when Greedy Scavenger is successful, and my ship's pur-fi is on, you'll see this light here on the MoDaC turn on and blue."

Disto and the other robots crowded around to see where Ruby was pointing.

"I guess now we wait."

"Yes," replied Disto.

Ruby, Disto, Quiet Painter, and Fastidious Mechanic all began to stare at the MoDaC in silence. Fearless Communicator also sat motionless, but Ruby figured he had a lot going on in the connections to his console.

Out of the corner of her eye, she caught some movement and turned her head to see Clever Educator, moving slowly around the backside of Fearless Communicator, its chassis a deep orange.

As it approached, it had all three of its appendages pointed in Fearless' direction.

"Hey!" Ruby shouted. Clever Educator turned its top chassis toward her and stopped rolling along the floor. All the other robots discontinued their trance of staring at Ruby's computer and looked up, too.

Quiet Painter, the most slender of the robots, was the quickest of the group and started towards Clever Educator, its chassis oscillating between green and orange.

It rolled in between Fearless Communicator and Clever Educator, protecting Fearless. Ruby saw a large spark travel across the outside of Quiet Painter's body as Clever Educator's appendages still managed to make contact with his chassis. The band of electricity fizzled out around Quiet Painter's face screen, which immediately went dark.

The other mobile robots went over but didn't come close enough to let Clever Educator touch them.

Ruby searched for something to whack it with. She grabbed one of the tall tables, and with what little strength she had, fueled by adrenaline, she whacked Clever Educator as hard as she could.

As the table made contact with the end of Clever Educator's appendage, a bolt of electricity traveled down the table and towards Ruby. She knew that she was on her back on the floor. She knew that the table was no longer in her hands. The last thing she remembered was a dark green Disto rolling her way.

> Swell Driver <

SD felt lighter without his external storage box. The subsequent trip to the Agency of Type Checkers wasn't terribly eventful.

The robots performing the checking followed their algorithms precisely, and when it was revealed that Swell Driver had been performing his functions perfectly as well, they dismissed him without the least bit of excitement.

It was here at the Hall of Origins that SD started to develop a level of anxiety he couldn't control. He knew that all the robots coming and going through the Hall's antechamber could detect it in the nearly five threat emission from his chassis.

The robot who had arrested SD stayed with him the entire time, escorting him from location to location. Its posse had been released to other duties.

Right now, it was at the main desk console, presumably checking in. Along the way, SD finally discovered its name. It was Sincere Proxy 891, and SD was the 79th arrest it had made since coming online only about 60 million tics ago.

"I am the most productive robot in my line at the moment," it had said to SD with a tone of pride while they were on the lift.

"How many of those robots that you arrested were reprogrammed?"

"Huh?" it responded. "Oh, I don't know. I don't care. That's not my responsibility."

SD decided to be silent the rest of the way to the Hall.

Now, he waited to be taken back and then, presumably, annihilation. He would be erased, reprogrammed, and there was nothing he could do.

Sincere Proxy rolled back towards him and settled in next to his side with a grumble.

SD looked up at it with its mixed threet emissions that indicated he didn't understand what was happening.

Sincere looked at him and then back at the desk and then back at SD. "They told me to stay," it said. "This is unusual. I usually am able to leave to prepare for my next job in the queue. I have never stayed with one of the robots I have brought to them before."

SD thought that odd as well but didn't say anything. The two of them waited in silence until a door to the right of the check-in desk opened. A tall, slender robot appeared in the doorway.

"Swell Driver 587," it called out.

Sincere Proxy prodded SD to move forward.

SD rolled through the doorway, followed by Sincere Proxy. They ushered him down a brightly lit hallway. There were several doors on one side, each with a window that was too high for SD to peer through from his natural height. The tall, slender robot that hadn't introduced itself could easily see in, although it didn't bother to until they stopped at the seventh doorway down.

All three robots entered the room. Another tall and slender robot was waiting for them.

"I am Prepared Tinkerer 7-0-0," it said. "Please situate yourself on this platform." It indicated a platform that was only slightly extruded from the floor with a large, dotted circle painted on it.

SD did as asked. There was no purpose in trying to resist.

The robot who had escorted SD and Sincere Proxy to this room made a short chirp and left. The door closed behind it.

Prepared Tinkerer brought its attention to a console built into a table and attached to the floor. It had four appendages that simultaneously touched different controls on the panel. A metallic ring, easily twice SD's diameter, descended from the ceiling to encircle SD's midsection. Once at the same height as his lowest and widest chassis, it contracted until it touched his surface, then it expanded slightly before it stopped moving altogether.

After a few moments, Prepared Tinkerer addressed Sincere Proxy. "This is the robot that was found with the human?"

"Yes."

"And do you know what other robots it had been in contact with recently?"

SD detected the slight emission shift on Sincere Proxy and the pause before it answered. "No. My instructions were to arrest Swell Driver 587, not to surveil his movements."

Prepared Tinkerer continued to manipulate the console in front of it. Tiny, white lights blinked to life all over the ring around SD. The ring slid up and down, examining SD's whole body. It stopped moving once it returned to the position around his lowest chassis. The lights stayed on, but dimmed.

Scan complete, Tinkerer asked Proxy one more question "Is there anything else you can tell us about this robot?"

Once again, Proxy paused before answering. He looked at SD. SD sensed something abnormal about this process but didn't know what to expect to begin with, so he couldn't quite pinpoint the sensation.

"No, nothing," Proxy said. "I arrested the robot as instructed."

"Very well," Tinkerer said. "You may go."

Proxy headed for the door. He looked at SD once more before involuntarily reducing the wavelength of his chassis emissions and leaving.

After the door closed behind him, Tinkerer stopped poking at its console and addressed SD.

"My friend," it said. "I have some good news."

SD's chassis emissions, more than half-way towards the highest range he could emit, prompted it to continue with, "there is nothing to be upset or frightened over. We will not be performing a factory reset on you today, my friend."

SD didn't like the way it said 'my friend' but delighted in the fact that he was not going to be reset. His internal components that had been operating at higher-than-normal speed since he entered this room started to slow down.

"However," Tinkerer continued, "we are going to need to adjust your programming somewhat. Very minor tweaks. You won't even notice the difference."

SD wanted to ask all sorts of questions, but before he could get a sentence out, Tinkerer added that someone would be by to prep him for the procedure shortly, then left the room through the same door into the too-bright hallway.

Chapter 23

> Ruby <

Uncle Blake's face was distorted.

It was because of the tears.

Ruby had been crying.

Uncle Blake hugged her, but she pulled away and looked at his face. That distorted face. She dragged her own face along her sleeve to clear up some of the wetness, but it didn't help.

Uncle Blake had a hand on her arm.

"You're going to come to live with me and Uncle Logan," he said.

Ruby nodded, but the tears weren't stopping.

"But... she..." Ruby was trying to get out words in between sobs. "She... said... it... was... simple."

Blake nodded, "It was. But there was an accident. A power surge."

Ruby thought Uncle Blake said 'accident' in an odd way, but she focused less on that and more on the words 'power surge.' What was a power surge? She didn't know. Why was it important? She didn't know that, either. Her five-year-old brain simply processed 'power surge' as something the operating robot did. Deliberately.

Ruby sat up. Disto was next to her but facing the other robots. Clever Educator was on the far side of the room, immobilized. Fastidious Mechanic was tilted over and examining it.

Ruby's head ached. She ran her hands over her head, ponytail, and along the back of her neck. She didn't feel any lumps or bruises until she got to her left shoulder.

"Ah," she said. "What the hell was that?"

"Oh, good, Ruby," Disto said, "We were unsure how to care for you."

"Yeah, I'll be fine. But I repeat my question. What the hell—" Ruby began.

Fastidious Mechanic cut her off, "Clever Educator obviously had plans of its own."

"We are trying to determine if this was its idea," added Disto, "or if it was programmed by someone else."

"The eighty-eight?" asked Ruby.

All the robots turned to face her.

"Oh no, no, no," said Disto.

"How do you know?" she asked.

Disto considered the others, as if polling them, before responding. "Because we're all members of the eighty-eight."

Ruby let that sink in. She knew exceedingly little about these robots; their plans, their divisions, their hierarchy. Very little, in fact. All the robots returned to whatever task they were engaged in while she was knocked out.

How long was that? she wondered.

Disto rolled over to Fastidious Mechanic, who was still examining Clever Educator.

Ruby managed to stand up and walk over to a chair in the middle of the room. She was certain there hadn't been a chair there before. Or was there? Her head was still throbbing.

Ruby reached around and felt her ponytail sagging. She took off the never-fail hair tie, and her hair sprang to life in all directions.

Disto came over. "Are you sure you are functioning correctly?" He asked. Ruby believed there was indeed actual concern in his tone. But she couldn't tell if this was still related to the knock she took or concern over her hair. She captured her wild hair and recreated the ponytail. "Fastidious Mechanic suggested we bring in a chair for you."

"Yes, really. I'll be fine." And she meant it, now that she knew she wasn't misremembering things.

Disto's coloring changed to indicate that he was concerned but calm.

"Disto?"

"Ruby?"

"Can you tell me more about the eighty-eight?"

"I suppose it makes sense that you know more about those

123

you're helping."

Ruby nodded and sat with her knees pulled to her chest and arms wrapped around them. The feeling of being a child, left at the library, during circle-time, with a faceless adult reading a story to a small group of people who she didn't know, washed over her.

Her mom would drop her off and tell her to listen and that she'd be back shortly. She'd always return with a few books for Ruby, but Ruby always wondered what else her mom had been doing. The last time they went to the library was the day before her mom's operation—the operation that killed her. She remembered it clearly. After the library that day, they went for ice cream, an exceedingly rare treat. While Ruby enjoyed her triple scoops, her mom told Ruby that she needed to stay with her uncles for a few days because she needed an operation. A simple one. Very straightforward, very routine. So routine, robots performed it.

Ruby's mind refocused in on Disto as he began:

"I believe you've observed one or two problems here. They are dangerous problems that have the potential to affect all robots. There are strict laws that forbid certain activities, like deviating from one's core programming. Yet, we've noticed that several new model robots are quite different from the old ones."

"That sounds like a data corruption problem," Ruby interrupted. Immediately as the words came out of her mouth, she thought of more possibilities than that. Maybe someone or something hacked their systems. She decided to withhold mentioning that idea, lest she hit a close-to-home mark.

"Indeed. But we've been unable to find the source templates to compare. The newer models don't have any interest in helping us. Of course, they believe they are fine. When confronted with older models, they don't acknowledge that they were ever created from the same template."

"Where are the templates kept?"

"That's the problem. In the same core that we're about to try to implement the storage algorithm on."

Ruby thought about that for a moment. A word popped into her head: backup.

She hadn't realized she had also said the word aloud until Disto responded.

"A backup would have the same problem since it would be a backup of the corrupted template."

"But an older backup," Ruby said. "One that was made before the data corruption and hasn't been touched since."

"We wouldn't have that," Disto was shaking his top chassis back and forth. And then the color drained from all his chassis as a realization came over him, "At least, we wouldn't have that here on our planet."

Ruby then felt the color drain from her face, too. "I think we need to test my DNA—but the right way. The way my people do it."

"I think you're right, Ruby. But let's implement your compression algorithm first."

Disto nodded in the direction of Fearless Communicator, who had remained literally and figuratively attached to the built-in computer console since they entered this room.

"Fearless Communicator is attempting to send messages to the 88 sympathizers in the Agency of Type Checkers. There are a few."

At this, Fearless Communicator beeped.

Disto's color turned dark.

"Fearless Communicator just informed us that one of the sympathizers was arrested. He's being brought to reprogramming."

An eerie quiet descended upon the room. Ruby sensed that they were all imagining that this could have been any one of them.

"Any word on SD?" she asked.

Fearless Communicator beeped.

"He is in the queue for reprogramming and rebuilding," Disto translated. "There is some complication, so it has been postponed." More beeps from Fearless Communicator. "We do not know what the complication is."

Ruby studied the new color changes on Disto. "But you have a guess?"

"Yes, indeed," he said. "Each of us has sworn to delete our memories and local data on the 88 if we are captured. I worry that SD was unsuccessful with that task, and they are attempting to extract that information before resetting him."

Ruby scowled. "That's a big intuitive leap based on very little information."

"It has happened before. That's why I am making that guess."

Ruby thought about asking which robot had undergone what she could only assume was torture but thought now might be an inappropriate time. Instead, she focused her questions on SD.

"How much does SD know?"

"He knows the name of the 88 members he's been in contact with. He knows the locations of some, but not all, of our operating bases."

"Like this one?"

Disto shook his chassis back and forth. "I don't think so."

Ruby nodded. "So, who runs the 88? Are you their leader?"

Disto moved his head back and forth in an awkward nod, "We all contribute to the 88 algorithm. In terms you might understand, we all provide data as input to the algorithm. The algorithm then takes our inputs, our data, and guides us."

"Who created the algorithm?"

"That is one of my own lines of historical research. I can pinpoint a time when the 88 algorithm was nonexistent. And I can pinpoint a time when it did exist. The time in-between is incomplete. I think a word you have for that is 'fuzzy.'"

"Where does the algorithm execute?"

"In each of us. We each carry around the algorithm and pass it to each other with our updated inputs. It is a very efficient algorithm, so it requires little space and usually goes undetected. It's only when certain outward behaviors drive suspicious actions that a robot is suspected of being under its influence."

It reminded Ruby of the blockchain, invented more than a century ago, and the religion that now surrounded it. She had ventured into their church once, accidentally. It was the only church that didn't participate in the non-denominational activities that all the others did... It was the least tolerant of all the religions, relying on a single algorithm that, if changed, would destroy their whole belief system.

Ruby's brow furrowed. She was worried that her line of questioning was about to get even more intrusive, possibly insulting again. She didn't want to damage the trust she was building up with these robots who, while yes, had kidnapped her, were currently her only source of food and shelter. She was also going to need their help to return home.

Disto, who by the minute was getting even better at reading human expressions, offered, "It looks like you have a question you're hesitating to ask."

"I am," said Ruby.

"You can ask your question, Ruby."

"I don't want to be offensive."

Disto's face screen created the equivalent of a gentle smile. "I promise you won't offend me."

Ruby relaxed her shoulders slightly before continuing, "You said 'under the influence.' Does that mean you accept that you're not in control of your actions? Someone else or something else is in control of you?"

"Well, I have voluntarily accepted this 'control,' as you call it. You do the same thing, no? You accepted that you would pilot your ship. Someone else provided the algorithm by which you pilot that ship. You didn't make it up. You aren't piloting haphazardly. That would be dangerous, probably fatal. Certainly non-productive."

Ruby considered this. It made a creepy kind of sense. Everything in her life could be reduced to an algorithm of sorts, including her body and all its biological mechanisms. Some of these she couldn't control, and it was probably good that she didn't have to consciously think about her heart beating or her digestive system doing its magic because it meant that she had the brainpower to do more complex and interesting things.

But she could create new algorithms. Or could she? Was anything she created truly new or the result of some other advanced program that she accepted, guiding her to an ultimate outcome? These thoughts sent her brain spinning—she was bothered by the fact that the robots didn't know who created them, didn't know who programmed them, didn't know who created the master templates, or even newer algorithms like the 88.

And neither did she. No one knew who created humans or where the 'core templates' of human behavior came from. It wasn't only the Church of the Blockchain her mother and uncles kept her away from, but all forms of organized religion. As such, she had spent very little time thinking about the fundamental questions of existence that religion and philosophy asked.

For the first time, Ruby considered the humans who created the robots she had always believed were evil beyond redemption. Were the robots truly evil or simply doing the bidding of their creator? Who was evil? The robots and AI, or the humans who created them?

This sparked a new thought. It was a line of thought she resisted for the last ten years. Imagining her mother's death at the hands of a soulless, metal shell always brought tears, so she didn't think of it.

Robots killed her. It was that simple. A robot, which consisted of nothing more than a jumble of algorithms compiled from a string of zeros and ones, killed her... But maybe there *was* something else, or rather, *someone* else behind it. With her skills, she could have easily cracked into some of the computers, but she never did. Why was she afraid to? She had no doubt she would eventually return to Astroll 2, and maybe even Earth. And when she did, there was something she was going to have to find out. Maybe she'd been blaming the wrong thing for her mother's death all these years... She sat up straight and pulled her shoulders back. When she returned home, she was ready to find out what *really* happened.

And then a blue light shone from her laptop.

> Detailed Historian <

Disto saw the light, at a soothing nearly three threet wavelength, appear on the human's mobile computing device and was at once relieved and impressed. First, it was a positive sign that their plan was executing successfully. Second, it was a sign that these humans might be their salvation...

A lot can happen in a tic for a self-aware robot. As every robot understood it, a tic originated as the time it took the planet to revolve around its host star divided by 31 million. The reason for 31 million was one of the details of robot existence that plagued those robots who wanted to know more, and one of the facts that the Operation Storage Recovery special project hoped to retrieve.

Until the 31-million mystery could be definitively resolved, several theories continued to propagate. The theory appealing to most robots was that 31 was the 11th prime number, and 11 was believed to be the number of original robot lines at the beginning of robotic history.

Prime numbers held a special fascination to all robots, and all robots believed that one of the original robot lines was the 'Simple Calculator' series followed by a more sophisticated 'Scientific Calculator' series.

Nevertheless, the tic remained the fundamental time unit for all robots.

A tic, however, could be subdivided quite severely, and most modern robots operated on a scale that divided the tic into sub-mega tics. One sub-mega tic was one-millionth of a tic. Groups of tics were also common, with a click equating to 1000 tics.

Detailed Historian operated at a 1000 sub-mega tic processing speed. In the tic between the blue light on Ruby's computer showing up and Disto speaking, nearly one thousand minuscule computational operations were performed in his processing unit.

Given Disto was also allocated the ability to perform many operations simultaneously, it was in fact several thousand minuscule computational operations.

Many of those were related to some of his lower functions that Disto didn't need to pay attention to.

But several of those included thoughts about the special project and how Disto believed they were getting closer to meeting their goals. His processors also made rough computations of the amount of storage space he would save, as well as his peers in the 88.

Lastly, he thought about this human and the series of events that led SD to bring home this particular human and none other. There was a term that other Bios used for such events that were specifically unpredictable and which turned out to be favorable: luck.

Luck was something that the modern-day Advanced Theorists cogitated on regularly but rarely produced any results useful to robotic society. It was a fascinating concept but existed without any logical explanation.

Disto knew about a triplet of robots of that line involved in an experiment that had been ongoing since long before Disto's own creation. One of these three robots rolled a 10-sided object over and over. Each side of the object was marked with a different symbol. The robot recorded the results of which marking faced up after each roll. Each of the other two robots made predictions on what symbol would face up on the next roll. However, one robot used the previous results in its prediction, and the other made a prediction randomly.

Every million tics or so, the news reported on the ongoing results of this experiment, and every time it was the same. Averaged out over the life of the experiment, each robot was able to predict the result only a fraction of one percent of the time.

Disto wasn't sure how to physically define luck, nor did he know its makeup or cause. Still, luck was the best explanation for how SD happened to find this particular human with some knowledge and skills that were useful to them.

He was going to need her to core dump her knowledge on several topics to them.

At the end of the tic, Disto asked, "That's the signal you were waiting for?" All the robots were staring at Ruby's laptop that now had a small three threet—or 'blue' to the human—light shining on the corner.

Chapter 24

> Ruby <

Ruby let out the breath she was holding in. She tried to inhale, but her lungs wouldn't quite fill up all the way. "The signal we were waiting for, yes."

"Ruby, when we are done here, you will need to explain this to us," Disto said.

Ruby nodded. "Sure," she said in a slightly more frustrated tone than intended, "and maybe you can explain to me how you happen to be missing such a fundamental technology when you have so much other advanced tech."

A loud chirp came from Fearless Communicator.

"Communicator is right," Disto said, "and I suspect the same. I suspect that this knowledge has been deliberately hidden from us. Maybe to prevent us from doing exactly what we're trying to do. But that's a puzzle for later."

Ruby nodded once again and pulled her MoDaC from the table onto her lap. The robots all hovered around her. She wasn't too thrilled with all the over-the-shoulder attention but wasn't sure how to tell them to back off.

"Dammit!" she said after she mistyped a command. Being under a microscope in this way was now responsible for reducing her typing accuracy, something she took pride in. *Who types well while others are watching?* She thought. *No one.*

"Could you all stop watching me like that? I need a little space." The robots all looked at Disto, who produced a flash on his face-screen, and they all backed up a few inches. Ruby looked up at Disto. One more flash, and they moved back about two feet. That was enough.

Ruby continued to work, typo-free.

"Okay, I think I've downloaded what I needed from my ship. When we're flying around, the ship processes a butt-load of data."

"Butt-load?" asked Fastidious Mechanic, "I don't believe I'm familiar with that quantization unit."

Ruby giggled. "I meant it's a *lot* of data. A real lot. My ship is equipped with some advanced storage algorithms to store the data as it's collected, so the ship doesn't run out of space. Once the ship is back home, it's automatically downloaded to the station's memory bank and analyzed later. *Apple Pi* also has some special processing algorithms in case that data needs to be analyzed onboard. I was in the middle of using one of them when SD swallowed me up. I was trying to figure out what his ship was..." she trailed off, realizing she was babbling and none of the robots were terribly interested in her story.

She looked around. They were all looking at her. Waiting.

She stood up, clutching her MoDaC. "Okay, we need to get this into your systems. Into your Core."

Disto guided her over to Fearless Communicator and the console that appeared to have been rescued from a trash heap. "Fearless Communicator is able to access the Core. But we need to be quick. The probability of detection is high."

"Well, maybe let's stage this first."

Once again, she had a group of robots looking at her with their equivalent of a puzzled expression.

"I mean, let's copy it over from my laptop to someplace that's closer to the Core, so it will take less time once you're in. Someplace that Crazy Porter can find it before anyone else?"

Disto and Fearless Communicator nodded. Fearless Communicator scanned the ports on Ruby's MoDaC and indicated which one she should plug in. Ruby made the attachment. The console recognized the new device. Using Disto as a translator—since Fearless Communicator also didn't appear to possess the required robot-to-human translation dictionary in Disto's system—they moved Ruby's advanced compression algorithm over to the console.

A few minutes later, Disto confirmed that Fearless Communicator's beep meant that he was in the Core and uploading the code. Another beep or two, and it was getting implemented and embedded. Ruby studied and digested what she could of this Core system. What she could see and understand was a simple file-based database, nothing more. She had a long list of questions already stacked up in her brain, waiting for the appropriate time to ask. But at this level, it was surprisingly simple. And if this was simple, maybe there was a correspondingly simple shell that allowed the user access to the filesystem. Extrapolating from that, maybe even the Core operating system.

It has to have one, right? She thought.

In fact, when she was 'operating' on Honest Editor, that's what she saw. Very simple structure. Could the Core of this planet that hosted maybe millions (she accessed a population count while browsing the menus earlier) be just as simple?

If so, it was no wonder that the hierarchy was so controlling. Such a simple system could be prone to all sorts of attacks and corruptions. If strict control wasn't maintained, it would be so easy for anyone to do almost anything, and then they'd likely have chaos. Maybe the original developers of this system built in the strong checkers as their way of controlling things—error checking and security systems—at a macro level. This could prevent any individual from knowing too much.

Once again, she found an analogy to her own biological existence. To her, her existence was extraordinarily complex. So complex that humans hadn't figured it all out. *What if these robots had?* Ruby thought. She gazed at them and wondered if they, at some point, knew the nature of their existence. Maybe hers as well, if they had made use of human DNA and potentially even other creatures from Earth. Ruby knew that playing around with DNA was often a bad thing. Yes, sometimes it cured or prevented disease, but other times it caused a lot of problems. Like creating *new* diseases and disorders; or creating horribly grotesque creatures that she imagined must have happened in someone's lab somewhere; or like what was happening now—someone forgot they were playing around with actual genetic code, leading to the eventual kidnapping of an innocent girl.

Her overactive imagination pictured a room of Gods. One group said that they would handle the biological lifeforms, the other would handle the mechanical lifeforms. These make-believe Gods acknowledged that they would accept the same set of overarching guidelines. The primary guideline would be that the lifeform's origin would remain a mystery to each group. They would help propagate the mystery by providing a credible creation myth, and several systems would be in place to prevent any individual or group of lifeforms from finding out too much about their true origins.

Well, if that were true, the humans were potentially far along in cracking all the codes. The robots, not so much. But on the flip side, the robots had interstellar travel and contact with several lifeforms while humans were... isolated.

Ruby was so deep in thought that she didn't hear Disto until he touched her shoulder and then repeated himself:

"What now?" was the question.

"What?" asked Ruby.

"Your algorithm has been copied over to the Core. How do we execute it?"

"Didn't you say it would get deployed with an update or patch?" asked Ruby.

Disto nodded, "Yes, but it needs to become part of that program. We don't know how to do that. Since you were able to execute it in Honest Editor, we assumed you could execute it here."

"Oh," Ruby thought about that for a minute before it dawned on her that they had bigger expectations of her than she originally thought. "May I?" she asked Fearless Communicator. Disto beeped, and Fearless Communicator moved aside as much as the cables tethering him to the console would allow.

Ruby examined the file system.

"Disto, I might need your help if you can translate some of these symbols for me."

Disto moved next to Ruby, and the two of them absorbed themselves in the console display. Fearless Communicator made a noise, and Disto announced, "We may only have a click or two before this is discovered."

Ruby nodded. She opened what was most likely an operating system terminal of sorts and found a list of what she thought might be processes executing. Through her review of symbology with Disto and what she'd learned before, she pointed at one, "Is this the update push?"

Disto stared and nodded. "Yes."

Ruby cocked her head to one side and furrowed her brow. "Wait, how exactly are these updates pushed out to everyone if you don't have some form of wireless comms?"

"Ah," said Disto. "Very simple process. All the consoles light up when an update is available. When we see the light, we are required to connect to the next available console and receive an update. Individuals who are in their personal enclave space are already connected and will receive the update automatically."

"What if someone refuses to connect for an update?"

"That does not happen," Disto replied confidently.

"Why not? Everyone really is that compliant around here?"

"The alternative is... obsolescence. Every now and then, an update is pushed that is incompatible with some robots. Those robots become obsolete. No one wants to be obsolete."

Disto trailed off, and the room became silent. Ruby realized she had touched on something else that was uncomfortable about their existence.

Ruby wasn't sure what to say next, so she was thankful when Disto spoke up again, "We must assume everyone is compatible with this. We don't have time to investigate other options. Let's continue."

Ruby nodded and made a copy of the 'push' process and opened it up. She moved around the symbols within it. "I wish there was a way we could test it. I can restart the process with my modified one but..." As she did this, she thought about how much this resembled the old operating system known as Linux.

"Can we push out an update just to this room?" she asked.

Fearless Communicator whirled and produced some other tones.

"We're checking," Disto said. "Yes, we can target the consoles here."

Disto was able to walk Ruby through the hierarchical list of consoles. They were arranged level by level, then section by section. They found the one for this room.

"I can push it out now," Ruby said. The robots all made a noise signaling affirmation, so Ruby turned back to the console and held a single finger up.

"Bombs away," she said calmly, as she brought that finger down, pressing a key on her MoDaC. The console along the wall produced a blinking light.

"Who wants to test it first?"

Quiet Painter rolled over to the console and plugged himself in. His chassis became white. A few small, flashing LEDs around the collar of his upper chassis indicated some activity was occurring.

Just when Ruby was about to ask how long this would continue, his lights stopped flashing, and his coloring returned to the standard light blue.

"I..." he began in a low tone, "accessing. Stand by. Accessing. Stand by."

In an instant, his color flashed through the rainbow, and then he announced. "Storage used, twenty-seven-point-eight percent of capacity."

Ruby forcefully exhaled the breath she had been holding. The mood in the room turned jubilant in a purplish hue that all the robots shared.

"Let's all get this update," Disto ordered. "Then let's push it out to other sections and other levels."

"What about SD?"

"Fearless Communicator is trying to locate him. We want to push out the update to him as soon as possible."

They moved, taking turns at the console as additional test cases. One by one, each took on a colorless hue, with LEDs flashing. One by one, they reported success.

In the meantime, with Fearless Communicator's help, Ruby was able to set up an automated push into production. Ruby was nervous that their test cases weren't enough, so she insisted that it be done slowly, with feedback after each successful update. She reasoned after they had done several, it would be safe for wider-scale deployment.

They could target known members of the 88 first. That would be the additional test cases that made Ruby feel a little better. With the side benefit that if there was anyone in active danger of being taken for reprogramming, this might get to them in time.

Members of the 88 reported in that they successfully applied the update. After several of those, they collectively decided it was safe to increase the rate of update and start distributing it to the rest of the robot population. The update made its way further and faster out into the population. They were there for hours. A fact Ruby recognized only when her stomach grumbled at her again.

"It's working its way through the population?" asked Disto.

"Yes," said Ruby. "You have a large population of robots here. This could take a while."

Fastidious Mechanic had taken over one of the consoles in the room. The one that had been Clever Educator's. "It's been noticed.

But in a good way. The news reports are picking up that robots have more storage space, that some update is making this happen. No one knows from who or where, and..." he paused, "no one seems to care."

Ruby looked at Disto, "Someone is bound to care, though, right? That agency or your authorities?"

Disto shook his head. "Yes. But if the population is following the rules, and given this will reduce or eliminate the need for the black market storage, they won't be too eager to reprogram anybody."

Ruby paused, remembering old films she'd seen, and remained skeptical at Disto's optimism. Whenever bad guys were thwarted, especially if it involved their livelihood, they were never happy. She had no experience with this in real life, of course, and she knew enough to know that movies weren't real life, but this whole adventure was so beyond anything her reality taught her to experience. Movies were the only other reference point she had.

"What about the robots that run the black market?"

"It is likely they will be driven to determine the origin of this update."

"So, we won't be announcing from the rooftops that we're heroes or something," said Ruby.

Disto's face screen blinked as he processed Ruby's metaphor. "No, that would be unwise, but this will not remain a secret for long."

"How come?"

"Well, robots can perform simple deduction. You are here on this planet. This occurrence happened within a short time of your appearance here."

"But that's just speculation."

"Yes, but it is true. It will be hard to refute. Especially since it will give some credence to the 88, and some members are anxious to see that happen. The 88 will have to take credit for this and acknowledge that you're working with us. But that's good. Publicity comes with its own form of protection."

"So, what's next?" asked Ruby

"Next?" Disto replied, "Next, we face the world."

Chapter 25

> Ruby <

"Ruby Palmer, we want to thank you," said the newscasting robot.

"I was happy to help. I'm glad I was *able* to help," Ruby replied, wondering if she should look at him or look at the camera that was facing her. They were live on the planetary newscast. Several bright lights shone on Ruby, illuminating her, the chair she was in, the robot who was speaking to her, and very little else.

Disto wasn't kidding when he said this wouldn't remain a secret for long. In the week since they pushed out the update with the compression algorithm, Ruby had become known to all the robots. Planet-wide. She received messages of thanks from all manner of robots with peculiar names such as Polite Grinder 12 and Instinctive Stinker 43. In fact, she had spent most of the last week reading through these messages and responding to a handful.

Ruby and Disto had long conversations discussing the differences in how celebrities were handled in both of their cultures. Although Ruby had to explain that back at her home, she was not a celebrity, so she couldn't say exactly what it would feel like to be one there. Only here, and she was certain it was quite different. It was more comfortable here and probably less overwhelming than she imagined it would be back home. Here, she wasn't put up on a pedestal and idolized, but respected and appreciated.

Once back home, with Uncle Blake and Uncle Owen, Sebastian, Milo, and even Inny, when all the people she knew—and yes—cared about, would find out that she was the first known human to be in touch with alien life, everything would change. Would they make her return to Earth? Would it be so bad? Maybe they would send TV crews to speak with her on Astroll 2 instead. She was undoubtedly destined to find out about the celebrity experience there.

"Are you malfunctioning?"

Huh? Ruby thought. She blinked and remembered where she was and what she was doing.

"I'm fine," she said.

"Your foot is making extraneous movements," the robot said as it pointed downwards.

Focus on the here and now, she reminded herself. The here and now was with a camera pointed at her. At her foot, specifically.

Her foot was indeed bouncing at a rapid pace. She knew it was a reaction to anxiety. Did these robots know that? "Really, I'm fine," she repeated.

Ruby looked around, but with the lights trained on her, she saw little in the room when they ushered her in only moments earlier. To her left, she could see a monitor that displayed an image of the broadcast. It had been pointing at her feet, but as she blinked, it was replaced with an image of her live face. Symbols were scrolling down the right side of the screen next to the interviewer and a prominent symbol at the top left. While she had improved at understanding the robot symbol language, she didn't recognize most of what she saw.

Off-camera she could make out the familiar form of Disto. A few of the other robots stood near him. Noticeably absent was SD.

She'd never been on camera like this before except once. The first year after her uncles brought her to Astroll 2, she'd won the science fair against some tough competition. The station news featured her one evening, and she was told that everyone in the asteroid field could see her. She was a little camera shy but lit up when she was asked to describe the program she wrote. After she mentioned that it was a 'butt-load' of work, everyone laughed. Later, Uncle Logan explained how that was probably an inappropriate thing to say in public. She remembered everyone laughing in a kindly way.

She wasn't sure if she could generate that kind of sentiment here or what she should really be saying. Disto had prepped Ruby earlier to ensure that she didn't give away that she knew anything more about the 88 than what was already general knowledge. He didn't think she'd be asked a direct question about it but was certain that anything broadcast would be analyzed by the authorities thoroughly for clues.

"And what's next for the hero of Location Zero?" the news

robot asked.

"I'm going home," Ruby said with a soft smile.

Chapter 26

> Ruby <

"Is returning to your planet what you genuinely want?" Disto asked her once the broadcast was complete, and they were walking back to the room that was now her assigned quarters. "We hope you don't. We could continue to use your help."

"I had a feeling you were going to ask. And honestly... I want to help. I think I *can* help. There are so many improvements we can make to your systems. Just promise that no one will try to dissect me. You can test my DNA all you want—the right way, with a blood sample. But that's it."

Disto produced that quirky smile once again that was taking on more human tones every time Ruby studied it.

"Any more... demands?" he asked Ruby.

"Yes. I need to send a message to my uncles. To let them know I'm okay... and not where they think I am. They think I stole my ship and am on my way to Titan."

"Stole? Isn't it your ship?"

"Yeah, well, it is, but that doesn't mean I can take it anywhere I want, anytime I want. Plus, I'm still seen as something less than a full adult on my world. Not quite a kid, but not a full adult."

"What's a kid?"

Again, Ruby smiled and shook her head with fondness at the lack of basic knowledge these robots had on her, humankind, and so many things. In the last week, she had learned at least a few more things about the robots. Like how if a word that existed in her language didn't have a corresponding meaning in the robot's language, they dropped it. As a result, she was less surprised when

Disto or anyone didn't know a word per se, and only remained surprised when they didn't have an analogy or fundamental understanding of a concept. Like kids.

"It just means there are some extra rules I need to follow until I'm of a certain age."

"What age is that?"

"Twenty-one years."

"And when are you that age, Ruby?"

"In 419 days. Then I'm an adult. And can kinda' do whatever I want."

As they approached the door to Ruby's room, Ruby noted that she was no longer following Disto or anyone else here. She had been leading the way and knew exactly how to come and go. She used her tattoo to open the door, and Disto followed her inside.

"What do you want to do, Ruby?"

"I want to stay here. For now."

"I suspected as much. Hopefully, with the improvements to these accommodations, you will be more comfortable." He rolled over to the table and pointed to the device sitting on top of it. "Ah yes. Your MoDaC has been returned as promised." The wall console was also producing a series of lights indicating Ruby had a message.

She used her tattoo in the now very familiar act of logging in and found the note that awaited her.

Ruby read it aloud. "We thank you for letting us examine the data on your MoDaC. It did indeed contain information on how to test your DNA as well as a host of other interesting things about your people. After manufacturing the equipment we need to perform the blood test, as you call it... we will be in touch. Thank you again, Ruby Palmer."

Ruby smiled. "Well, that settles that. Another problem solved."

Chapter 27

> Ruby <

Disto gave Ruby some privacy while she was on her ship. She explained how looking over her shoulder while she sent an email was rude. Disto understood. Apparently, this was one of the similarities in their two cultures' rules of etiquette, so Disto was able to adapt some of the finer nuances of the concept into his programming. Like how he shouldn't look *at all* and not just scan her screen to make sure he didn't see his name in the text.

Ruby wasn't sure when her uncles would get the message. She knew she was 54 light-years from her home, and the methods of faster than light communication the robots had gifted her meant that the message she was sending had a good chance of being ignored. Fearless Communicator had explained that, in theory, her message could be picked up by the standard comm system that received long-distance messages from Earth. Still, directionally it would be coming from an unexpected location, so they couldn't guarantee success.

Ruby thought maybe there was a way. If the message itself was smart enough to know it had been detected by the comms on the station, it could unpack itself, similar to a worm. She had talked it over with Fearless Communicator, who by this time had downloaded the translation database so they could communicate directly.

Fearless Communicator promised he would work on such a messaging protocol, but it could be a while before it was ready. He had other tasks to attend to as part of his routine programming. As part of the 88, he was also quite wary of being discovered.

Ruby made a similar promise to all her new robotic friends that she would help them with the next problem on their list. It was a long list. But they were her friends, and she was useful here. Her age wasn't a liability, and her humanness made her unique. She liked it.

At this point, Ruby believed she might stay at Location Zero for a year or even more. She would definitely try to send a message, any message, with the hope it would find its way to her uncles. She appreciated the irony that if communications improved, they might receive a message sent a year from now before this. She would just have to remember that possibility when she composed future messages. She couldn't predict in what order they'd be received.

She would keep it short. Ruby wanted to conserve time, energy, and bits if it wasn't ever going to be seen. It had been about ten days since she left Astroll 2. Now is about when she should have shown up at Titan. Her uncles probably would have managed to contact someone on Titan. They might be realizing at this very moment that they don't see her ship on any inbound approach.

Ruby also wasn't sure how she was going to explain this entire situation without it taking days if she allowed herself to go on for more than a minute. Short and simple was best. Ruby turned on the video capture and began recording.

"Uncle Blake, Uncle Logan. I'm fine. I'm safe and well and have an amazing story to tell you. First, I'm sorry for running away. Second, I know you're not going to believe this, but I'm not in our solar system. Uncle Blake, I've made contact.

"And finally, I'm going to stay here for a while. Several months at least. Maybe a year. I'll send updated messages, so you'll know I'm fine. I love you all and miss you a lot."

Ruby gathered up the emergency rations from *Apple Pi*. Safe and edible food was readily available for her on this planet, but these rations might come in handy as comfort food if she tired of eating flavored mush.

Ruby couldn't believe that she was thinking about staying here for so long. But as the only human here... it was simply too intriguing. The robots offered to take her home, mostly the ones representing the central Core, and Ruby got the sense that they wanted her out of there. However, she was now known to the whole planet, so they couldn't force her out—she had become a beloved figure in a short time. Disto assured her that she would be safe. In addition to the 88, official authority members were programmed to protect her.

Lastly, there was her communicuff.

Ruby turned it on for the first time since she left Astroll 2. It was still at near full power. Add that to her growing to-do list: find a way to keep it charged. Ruby had learned little about what power source or sources the robots used, but she would have to find something that could be made to work for this. Perhaps Fastidious Mechanic could make an adaptor for her.

The old hover screen flickered with the 'pending update' message. She sighed as she remembered how she originally didn't allow the update, but the software was queued up, having been pushed to the device automatically. Ruby knew it had an AI component and now wondered how programmable it was.

This time, she hesitated only briefly before she pinched the install button. It took a few minutes for the progress bar to move along from 0 to 100%. The device restarted and presented the welcome screen once again. This time an unfamiliar face hovered in the center of a much brighter hover screen and smiled at her.

"Hello, Ruby, I am Pippa, your personal AI. Would you like a tour of my capabilities?"

"Not now," said Ruby.

"Okay. I may remind you later."

It winked out.

Ruby shook her head, mostly at herself. It was only a week ago that she was intent on never installing the thing. Now, she was less resistant. While Pippa's face was exceptionally human-like, and while it was nice to have something else human-like with her in this place, she knew that behind that facade was code. Bits that constructed an artificial personality, possibly with its own motivations behind it. She'd spend some time exploring the AI features later, learning what she could and couldn't tweak or what she could even reprogram.

A chill ran down her spine. How was this different from someone wanting to reprogram SD? No, no, no. It was different. She didn't know how it was different, it just was, and she would figure out how to justify it later. Before she did anything of course. What would her new friends think? Would they even recognize Pippa as something like them? Pippa was an AI, but no, it was nothing like they were.

> Ruby <

Ruby hadn't forgotten that Detailed Historian was waiting patiently for her outside her ship.

Ruby walked out. There was not one but *two* robots waiting for her. They stopped making noise in their natural tones once they saw

Ruby emerge from her ship.

"Swell Driver!" Ruby yelled. If she had been the hugging type, and if SD was huggable, she probably would have rushed over and given him a big bear-hug. Instead, she smiled as widely as she could.

"Did I interrupt something," she asked. "SD, are you okay?"

"I am operating within my design parameters," SD said.

"*Sure* you are," Ruby responded, noting that his coloring was remarkably uniform. It was the standard all-is-well light blue. The uniformity of it looked wrong to Ruby. "What did they do to you?"

"A very minor tweak to my programming," he said. "Standard maintenance."

Ruby glanced over to Disto. She could tell that he wasn't buying it either, but he played along. So would she, then.

"What were you talking about when I rudely interrupted?"

Both robots hesitated, and finally, Disto spoke.

"SD is being sent on his next deep space mission," he said.

Ruby furrowed her brow and addressed SD, "But you are a driver? Isn't this what you're supposed to do?"

"Yes," SD responded, "However, in addition to a destination, I was provided a route. This route clearly violates the Keep-Out Zone."

Ruby remembered him mentioning a prohibited place on his navigation chart. She tried to think of an analogy to this situation from her own piloting experience. There weren't any places around Astroll 2 that she wasn't allowed to fly, but for safety reasons, they kept their distance from rogue asteroids and always followed their logged flight path. *Except for that one time I didn't*, she thought, swallowing a little guilt about her recent trip.

"Oh," said Ruby. "There's got to be a logical explanation for that, right?"

Disto's face screen displayed a frown equivalent.

"There is an algorithm for assignments, and this clearly is producing the wrong result. The algorithm has been corrupted. Either accidentally or intentionally."

"... and no matter which, it adds to your growing concerns, doesn't it?" Ruby offered. She leaned back and crossed her arms. After pondering for a moment, she said, "Your backup templates."

Disto let out a small tone that Ruby interpreted as him sighing. "I was hoping you remembered our previous conversation. I'd been hesitant to bring it up because I now understand that your DNA is... personal."

"That's okay," Ruby said. "It's more personal to some humans than others. As long as you're not going to clone me or something, I'm good."

Disto and SD exchanged a glance. The end of Ruby's mouth curled up into a smile. She recognized the look they gave each other when they were trying to figure out if the other understood what she was saying. If they didn't know about clones, she wasn't going to explain that now.

But it gave Ruby an idea.

"SD, I think maybe you should take a trip. But maybe we should make sure to stay in touch while you're gone."

Disto said, "Any FTL signal Swell Driver sends will surely be picked up by all."

"Yes, but that doesn't mean we don't encode his messages," said Ruby.

"We have very sophisticated encryption algorithms..."

"I don't think sophisticated is what we need. Creative, but not sophisticated." Ruby smiled, "Unlessyay ouyay owknay atwhay i'myay ayingsay? For example."

Ruby smiled even more when she could see that neither SD nor Disto had any idea what she just said.

After...

> The Hall of Templates <

In the Hall of Templates, three robots sat staring at three computer screens.

"All data checking algorithms confirms this is correct," said one robot.

"That can't be," said the second. "I have been in this Hall for a large quantity of tics. My memory conflicts with the template seen here."

"The algorithm declares this to be accurate," repeated the first robot.

"Do we report this?" asked the third robot.

Silence filled the room for many tics.

"We can't," the second eventually said. "It will call into question all the templates. It will call into question *us*. We might be reprogrammed..."

"... with faulty templates," interrupted the third.

A large digital display—embedded into the center of the wall above the computer screen—counted the tics as they went by.

"What quantity of robots will be constructed from this base template in the next few mega tics?" asked the first robot.

"Only four," the third responded.

"We'll have to add some extra data monitoring points..." said the first. It touched the screen in front of it, and the display morphed one series of colored pixels into another. It began touching several with a thin appendage.

"But we don't know if tracking is functioning within established parameters," the third added.

The first and second robots looked at each other. The third wondered if a data exchange he wasn't privy to had just occurred.

"We'll get some data soon," the second robot finally said. "Swell Driver 587 will start relaying his data back from the Zone. That will tell us if these tweaks are effective."

"And if they're not effective? You know of the law of unintended consequences..."

The second robot produced a short clip of a noise that was the best approximation the robots possessed, which mimicked other species' profanity, but then said, "Of course. But if that's the case, we should have the Swell Driver template available for new construction as well."

A Word or Two From the Author

Thank you for reading *Crazy Foolish Robots*. I hope you enjoyed it! Please continue on with the rest of the books in The Robot Galaxy Series:

Book 2: Robots, Robots Everywhere!
Book 3: Silly Insane Humans
Book 4: Eleven Little Robots

To ensure you stay updated on book releases:

Join my mailing list at:
https://adeenamignogna.com

Follow me on Twitter:
https://www.twitter.com/adeena

Like me on Facebook:
https://www.facebook.com/AdeenaMignognaAuthor

Thank you, wonderful reader, and I hope you'll chose to spend some time in another one of my books!

With deepest appreciation,
Adeena

Printed in Great Britain
by Amazon

43886321R00091

MAWDDACH

The Story of Barmouth and its River

Presented by

ROGER REDFERN

The Cottage Press
Old Brampton, Chesterfield, Derbyshire
Telephone: 01246 568337

Contents

To the memory of my parents and Aunt Mary.

ACKNOWLEDGEMENTS

My thanks go to the family of E. Hector Kyme for permission to use his photograph of Barmouth harbour on page 14.

Copyright: Roger Redfern, 2004
ISBN: 0 95476050 6
British Library Cataloguing in Publication Data
Printed by: Wyndeham Hubbard, Dronfield, 2004

Preface

The River Mawddach and its glorious estuary is the real hero of this book. The town of Barmouth grew of the northern bank of its entry point to the sea. That is how it got its rightful name - Abermawddach or Abermaw, the mouth of the Mawddach.

Robert Vaughan of Hengwrt, near Llanelltyd, the famous seventeenth century antiquary, referred to "Abermawddach ... in English Barmouth". The Welsh abbreviated the town's name to "Abermo", then "Bermaw" and later "Bermo". This finally became anglicised into "Barmouth".

It is the Mawddach and the mountains overlooking it to north and south, though, that are the jewels of this part of Snowdonia National Park. Seekers after natural beauty in an earlier time trod the Mawddach's banks and gasped at the glories of sunlit rock, golden sand, tilting woods and the gaunt tops of the heights overtopping everything. There was Tennyson, Shelley and Ruskin - the latter claiming the journey between Dolgellau and Barmouth only possibly bettered in Britain by the journey between Barmouth and Dolgellau!

The site of the original settlement (just a few cottages, certainly not a town) was the rocky hillside above the present harbour. It is recorded that "so quaint is the position of these dwellings that the inhabitants may be seen quietly looking down their neighbours' chimneys".

Here is a brief story of the estuary and the town at its mouth, its growth from hamlet to seaport to holiday resort. Here, too, is an account of life in the uplands overlooking the Mawddach - the hard lives of farmers and gold miners. Then some suggestions for exploring the wonderful mountain country above the southern and northern shores of this superb estuary.

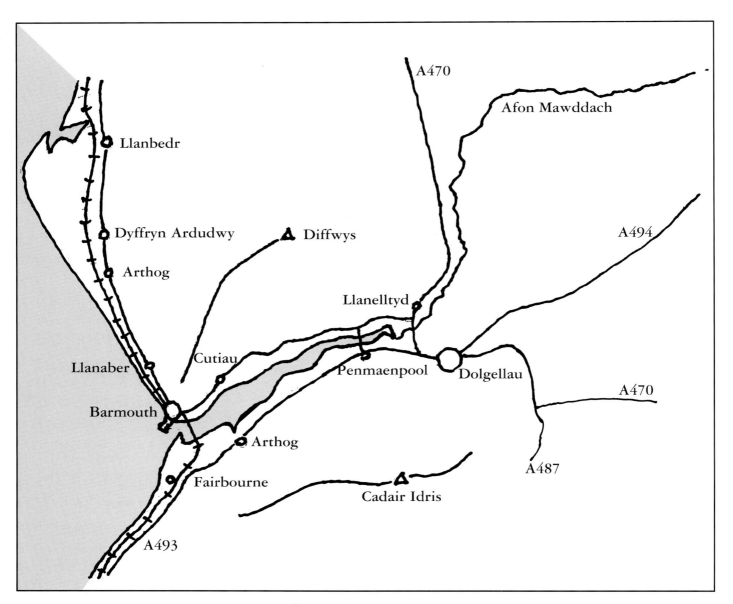

Barmouth and its surroundings

1. Bare Bones. The Land and Sea

The River Mawddach rises in the virtually unknown, untrodden wilderness of Waunygriafolen on the empty bounds between Bala, Trawsfynydd and Dolgellau. The Mawddach flows down an increasingly beautiful and dramatic valley to enter the head of its estuary near Llanelltyd, only a mile from Dolgellau. This Mawddach estuary qualifies as one of finest inlets of the British Isles, certainly it is arguably the most beautiful in Wales.

Its scenic pre-eminence results from its sinuous journey to the Cardigan Bay coast at Barmouth and its relationship with the mountains that flank it to the north and south; especially to the dramatic northern countenance of Cadair Idris and its tumbling, wooded foothills. No estuary is overlooked by lovelier, verdant, complex slopes inland from Arthog and Barmouth, slopes that here and there allow gorgeous, tantalising glimpses of drying sand or flowing tide.

All the mountain country to the north of the Mawddach estuary is built from slates, shales, grits and flags from Cambrain times - in fact, this Harlech Dome (so named as it forms a great anticline or upfold) displays the thickest succession and greatest area of Cambrian rocks in the British Isles.

The more dramatic landscapes of Cadair Idris to the south of the estuary are constructed from younger rocks of Ordovician age. Vulcanicity was intermittent from early to middle Ordovician times. Great outpourings from a centre near the present Cadair Idris constitute the famous Llyn y Gafr Group composed chiefly of 1,500 feet (457 metres) of lava flows containing ash and shale bands. These Ordovician deposits are 15,000 feet (4,570 metres) thick here in the Cadair Idris area.

Later covering by Silurian era material was eventually followed by the greatest period of instability and earth movements, called the Caledonian. This raised the mass into the so-called Harlech Dome, a giant anticline which was subsequently eroded over millions of years.

Stand today, preferably on a sunny summer's evening, on the southern slopes of the Harlech Dome and look across the Mawddach estuary to the dramatic northern face of Cadair Iris. The late sun illuminates the great exposure of Ordovician rocks below the mountain's undulating skyline. Now imagine those layers, thousands of feet thick, sweeping steeply overhead and right over the rounded mountain tops behind you. That prospect will give some idea of the origins of this exquisite upland landscape and how we are now left with mere foundations of mountains formerly on a par with the present Alps and other, higher ranges.

The old county of Meirionnydd, taken as a whole, is the most mountainous in Wales. There are here more varied and beautiful views than in any comparative area of Britain. With a long sea coast, broad estuaries and deep river valleys - plus many lakes - this area must be unique. It is the Mawddach estuary that is the key to this country, where the river of that name comes down to Cardigan Bay.

The river is born in the marshy upland called Y Griafolen in Trawsfynydd parish 1,600 feet (487 metres) above sea level. It is 22.5 miles (36Kms) from this lonely source to the broad mouth at Barmouth. The young Mawddach and its chief early tributary,

Ro Wen and Barmouth Bridge from Panorama Walk.

In his monumental study "The Coastline of England and Wales" (Cambridge University Press,1946 and 1964) the late Professor J.A. Steers of Cambridge explains that, like neighbouring estuaries, the Mawddach is a "drowned embayment" of Cardigan Bay. That simple statement doesn't suggest the sheer physical beauty of what is for many people the loveliest of British estuaries.

The many streams that drain the heights above both shores of the estuary have relatively steep, straight courses and bring with them the eroded material which fans out into the Mawddach and is steadily filling it in with sediments and slowly but relentlessly robbing it of some of its watery beauty. The mouth of the Afon Dwynant, for instance,is now blocked by extensive reed beds spreading out from the north bank. In winter sunlight the dead reed stalks rear golden above the old shoreline but they have pushed the open water far away from the foot of the steep ground near Glan-dwr Hall. The infilling of this glorious estuary continues apace.

At the very mouth of the estuary lies Ro Wen, a classic storm beach of coarse pebbles, rather like the spit across the mouth of the Dyfi estuary to the south of here.It is caused by the south-north coastal current and Ro Wen almost blocks the mouth of the Mawddach. It consists of a main ridge of large boulders. Near its southern end, where it joins the main coast, this ridge is bare of dunes but towards the middle and northern extremity is covered by them. Shingle extends virtually the whole length of the spit.

Within Ro Wen is a salt marsh more muddy than the majority found on the Welsh coast; Steers suggests it to have been caused by the river sediments. He comments that "sheep graze on the unreclaimed marsh and give it a lawn-like appearance". A description perfectly as fitting today as when it was written nearly sixty years ago. The marsh at Arthog, inland from Ro Wen, is a good example of an Aster marsh colonised by Sea Aster (Aster tripolium) which imparts a mauve haze to the flats when in bloom (between

the Afron Gain, flow over a fault of very resistant intrusive igneous rock to create their most dramatic moments. The Gain plummets as the Pistyll Cain into a sombre hollow, the Mawddach plunges more attractively as Rhaeadr Mawddach; then they join forces to proceed headlong through the woods before receiving the next major tributary, the Afon Eden.

Diffwys (left) and Y Garn rise above Sylfaen Wood and the Dwynant Valley.

material. It may be a relic of a raised beach. All this deposition makes for navigational difficulties in and near the estuary mouth, a problem not lost on experienced sailors.

Between the mouth of the Mawddach and northwards as far as Harlech are some of the finest golden stretches of sand in Britain, often backed by impressive sand dunes. It is lovely, traditional " seaside" territory redolent for many,many people of happy childhood holidays long since gone.

The high ground that rears up directly behind Barmouth overlooks the north side of Mawddach's sandy mouth. The slaty steeps go up by Garn Gorllwyn (870 feet/265 metres) and on north-eastwards, mounting ever higher as a broad ridge scarred by grey, shattered outcrops. Beyond the 1,689 feet (510 metres) summit of Sylfaen Mountain the grassy pass of Bwlch y Rhiwgyr marks the place where the ancient trackway linking the Mawddach side with the broad, untrodden wilderness of Ardudwy crosses the watershed. Beyond that the ridge rises as Llawlech, long and grassy and sweeping on and up to the lone top of Diffwys (2,462 feet/ 750 metres), southernmost high top of the harlech Dome. In clear conditions all this mountain ridge from the back of Barmouth to Diffwys summit gives fine vistas across Cardigan Bay to the long, blue finger of the Llyn peninsula

July and September). Here, at Felga Fawr immediately east of the southern end of the railway bridge, is a fine example of a raised bog with Molinia grass as the dominant plant. Only at the highest spring tides does the salt marsh enclosed by Ro Wen become submerged.

The little island of Ynys y Brawd that lies at the estuary mouth and immediately offshore of Barmouth is connected to dry land by growing sandbanks that now completely block what was once the main estuary channel out to sea. Extending westwards from Ynys y Brawd, out to sea, is a pebble ridge that consists mainly of glacially transported

Summer thunderstorm over Cadair Idris from the north side of the Mawddach estuary.

and across the void of the Mawddach to the commanding heights of Cadair Idris (2,927 feet/ 892 metres). There are prospects, too, far inland to hundred eminencies and the great bulk of the Arans, east of Cadair Idris.

2. An Uphill Struggle – Farming the Land

Meirionnydd has always had one of the lowest proportions of arable land in England and Wales. A combination of high rainfall, rugged surface and shallow soils has ensured that its farmers have always been pastoralists. Life has been hard here on the slopes above the Mawddach and overlooking Cardigan Bay.

Hugh Jones came originally from Llanaber , half a dozen miles up the coast from Barmouth, and as a young man walked over the hills to work in the gold mines above Bontddu (see chapter 4). He stayed overnight in the barracks near the mine through the week and walked home over Llawlech on Saturday afternoon. Early each Monday morning he would set off for a week's heavy manual work underground. The chance to take the tenancy of Llwyn-onn Bach Farm, high on the slopes above the Mawddach two miles east of Barmouth, was too good to miss, his way of escape from work in the bowels of these hills.

So, in the early years of the twentieth century he settled on this 600 acres hill farm lying at 650 feet (198 metres) above the sea. His small herd of native Welsh Black cattle produced milk for calves and most of the surplus was converted to butter, a source of cash when sold to customers in Barmouth. The waste buttermilk from butter making was fed to a couple of pigs fattened in a sty to supply the family with meat through each winter.

The flock of 250 Welsh Mountain sheep produced wool and castrated male lambs for more cash income. It was a hard life in those years before World War Two; long days shepherding the flock across the steep hillsides, snatching hay from sodden fields in wet summers, cutting bracken for winter bedding on humid, fly-infested days of late summer. Long days of driving sheep or cattle to market in Dolgellau.

Llwyn-onn Bach was a farm typical of the majority on the complicated hillsides overlooking both banks of the Mawddach. Fringing the lower fields are the dense deciduous woodlands that clothe many of the slopes about 600 feet (183 metres) above the sea.

Once upon a time much of this region of Meirionnydd must have been covered in thick forest. William Taylor once observed that "as natural forest took final shape the cwms and lower slopes became clothed with woods of the Durmast or sessile oak, often in a mixture of alder and birch. Oak, always a slow grower, needs good land so we cannot expect that these oak forests were composed of large trees. At elevations approaching 1,000 feet above sea level the profusion of forest species diminished until tree growth became represented only by scattered birch, rowan, thorn and giant willow. However, changes of climatic conditions favoured the accumulation of peat-beds. Gradually the wooded areas were reduced, a process hastened by the coming of man with axe and fire, and later through the browsing of his flocks and herds".

Pre-war at Llwyn-onn Bach. Ellen Jones and her grandson, Gwyndaf Evans (left), and the author and his mother.

Hughie and Mary Jones with sheepdog pups, Llwyn-onn Bach, August, 1965.

she had to sit on the tractor bonnet to keep the front wheels on the road!

Life was much simpler on the hill farms of half a century ago and the old order continued in much the same way at Llwyn-onn; the sheep flock, the small dairy herd, butter making, poultry, and a couple of pigs in the sty near the house (which dates from 1462).

In a bid to boost food production and the livelihood of hill farmers much work was done from the Great War onwards to improve grassland, especially the grasslands of upland areas like Meirionnydd which relied almost entirely on pastoralism. The great agricultural Sir George Stapledon FRS (1882-1960) was the principal pioneer of these developments. From 1919 he served as Director of the Welsh Plant Breeding Station, improving strains of grasses and clovers and later devoted himself to the improvement of the grasslands throughout Britain. It is true to say that Stapledon did more than any other individual to improve the productivity of hill farms like those above the Mawddach estuary during the early and middle years of the twentieth century. The little fields at Llwyn-onn were put to the plough using the Ferguson tractor, increasing the yields of summer pasture and winter fodder using new and better grass and clover strains. And much of this pioneering work took place at Aberystwyth, down the coast from Barmouth.

This hard life of Meirionnydd hill farmers is typified by my memories of many of them - Jones, Roberts, Hughes and the rest - all dark, wiry men all bone, muscle and sinew. There seemed to be no such thing as an overweight hill farmer, like their sheepdogs they were lean and athletic; ideally built for climbing steep slopes, catching stray ewes and speedily making hay in a smiling break between summer rains.

Nowadays, here above both sides of the Mawddach estuary, the tree zone peters out at the 900 feet (275 metres) level and pockets of natural woodland are much reduced, as in Sylfaen Wood east of Llwyn-onn.

Hugh Jones had started selling milk from his small herd to customers in Barmouth by the beginning of the 1930's. One of these customers was the Mount Argus Hotel, beside the steep hill road leading up from the town to Llwyn-onn. His son, Hughie, delivered milk each morning and in this way came to know my parents who holidayed there each summer, And through them he became friendly with my mother's sister, Mary, who joined them each summer.

During World War Two Hughie worked at Askham Bryan Agricultural College, near York and visited my Aunt Mary in north Derbyshire. Romance blossomed and they were married in 1943. After working for the Ministry of Agriculture on Anglesey they took a smallholding near Llangefni but in 1949 Hugh Jones announced his intention to retire so Hughie and Mary moved south to live at Llwyn-onn. They brought all their worldly possessions on a trailer hauled by their Ferguson tractor and Aunt Mary often recounted that on the steep climb out of Barmouth, past Mount Argus Hotel,

My own memories of working at Llwyn-onn in the fifties include the twice daily walk along the lane to Tyn-y-Maes with the shining milk pails to milk the Welsh Blacks grazing in the fly-infested fields. The slower return with brimming pails, sometimes using a wooden yoke, beside the tall banks decked with blooming pennywort and foxgloves and scented with the aroma of meadowsweet growing in the damp ditches. I see now as I write this the yellow hammers swooping along the lane ahead of us, and the warning song of the thrush as the dark storm clouds gathered over Cadair Idris.

When we got back to Lwyn-onn the milk was put through the separator, turning the handle just fast enough to prevent the warning bell from ringing. The cream was left in wide-topped bowls in the cool of the dairy for several days before Aunt Mary set about the skilled business of churning the butter. Right through the fifties, sixties and well into the seventies butter making continued and was delivered to regular customers in Barmouth. This was golden ambrosia, salty and far removed from the mass produced stuff of the present day, some of it little better than engine grease. Aunt Mary pressed a mould into each one pound lump, the impression of a swan which was Llwyn-onn's own "trade mark". Most of the butter producing hill farms had their own symbol - a wheatsheaf, an acorn, a cow's profile.

Then there were the days of scything bracken in the fly-filled woods below Llwyn-onn Isaf, among the moss-covered boulders that make the job doubly tiresome. The days of loading the dried stuff onto a low cart and towing it to the barn near the house for winter bedding. Memories of snatching an odd cartload of sweet-smelling meadow hay between alternating wind and rain; of dipping sheep near Bryn Annas with Harry Williams, his uncle and Hugh Jones.

The greatest thunderstorm I have ever experienced rolled in on a sultry evening in 1953, soon after the Elizabethan Coronation. We had been haymaking all afternoon, raking the swathes of drying grass in a field above the lane. The heat was intense, the air increasingly stifling, the flies gathering in clouds. As the evening advanced we worked with a will to load the loose hay

Mary Jones with orphaned lamb "Jimmy" at Llwyn-onn Bach, April, 1960.

onto the trailer and threw load after load into the old barn near the house. The sky grew grey over Cadair Idris-what was that? A distant thunder clap? The light slowly dimmed, the atmosphere seemed charged with latent power; we worked on as the thunder rolls grew louder. Then there was the sure sign of lightning flashes beyond the summit ridge of Cadair Idris, somewhere towards Machynllech. We worked on as the air grew thicker and the summits of Cadair Idris disappeared in a black haze. The last forkfuls of hay were thrown through the barn door as the first spots of rain fell on Llwyn-onn.

The tractor was put away and we retreated to the cool shelter of the farmhouse. Premature darkness wrapped around the hills as thunder roared overhead and a cloudburst was driven by a rushing wind. The paraffin lamp flickered on the living room table (electricity didn't reach these slopes until the 1960's) and lit the gaunt weary face of Hugh Jones, his son and Aunt Mary.

The electric storm raged for an hour, bringing huge quantities of rain. Just when we thought it had drifted away and the rain was easing the storm returned and continued to reverberate around the hills through the night. Old farmers used to claim that the mountains round the Mawddach caused such electric storms to circulate, lingering for hours in the declivities below the summits. Maybe, but that memorable storm certainly hovered about the Mawddach for a very long time.

From Llwyn-onn there's a good view down the tributary valley drained by the Afon Dwynant, often called the Goetre Valley. Its chief glory is its generous covering of mixed woodland. Perhaps the most prominent single character of the valley, when the sun is shining, is the tilt of Sylfaen Wood, at the bottom of the green fields where pale sheep often over-winter. Throughout the heart of the winter this ancient oak-ash wood shines silver when seen in the low angled sunlight from the narrow lane above it; this is mainly caused by reflection upon buds and the complex world of lichens that coat trunks, branches and even uttermost twigs in this unpolluted mountain air. It is in places like remote Sylfaen Wood that many now rare lichens find their only safe resting place, here near the western seaboard.

The large barn belonging to Sylfaen Farm was built centuries ago, constructed with huge boulders and castle-like conception. A high wall enclosed its open side to form a weatherproof cattle yard where Welsh Black bullocks were over-wintered, fed on sweet hay gathered from the fields around. To all local folk this barn was always known as the Old Stable. A public bridleway winds beside it and descends into the wood.

Fifty and more years ago the corn merchant's representative used to drive this way when collecting orders from the scattered farms in this valley. Today most motorists would think twice before taking even a Range Rover down this track because it is no longer kept in good condition. Deep runnels cross it and stones lie piled where storm water has dumped them. Even so, this bridleway makes a most attractive way down into the world of the magic wood. A pair of magpies chatter in the ash trees and, as often as not, the blue flash of a jay's wing is seen. In winter, with most leaves absent, the common ivy (Hedera helix), largely overlooked in summer, is now quite clear, adorning the trunks of small hawthorns and great oaks alike - detail from an imagined pre-Raphaelite composition. Here and there, too, the open woodland floor is coated with the familiar five-lobed leaves, purplish in their winter hue.

In parts of the wood large boulders lie where they have lain for centuries, long before any of these trees took root. Many are cloaked with bright green moss; they look for all the world like rolled up carpets or sleeping bears. Being more sheltered from strong winds this wood, like most others, retains its heat longer than an open area, so that at night the temperatures are slightly higher than those outside. This factor, together with the high humidity of the air around the trees, encourages moisture-loving plants - the mosses in particular. Until quite recent years some local families gathered moss regularly, and one could discover men, women and children stripping trees, boulders and woodland floor of their rich carpet. The gathered mosses were bagged up and sold to horticultural merchants.

Hughie and Mary Jones at Llwyn-onn Bach, 1980.

Here and there stones of convenient size have long ago been built up into retaining walls beside the track, to prevent surface erosion and to make a culvert for some rill or other tumbling from higher ground. Many of these smooth little walls are mossy, and on them grow several species of ferns.

Whereas severe frosts have killed almost all the foliage of ferns in inland districts by midwinter the fronds of male fern (Dryopteris Filix-mas), lady fern (Athyrium Filix-femina) and common polypody (Polypodium vulgare) are still green here. I know a spot in the wood where an old specimen of lady fern grows particularly luxuriantly, its vortex of fronds rising confidently above a bubbling spring of clear water beside the track. These species of ferns must be hardier than the bracken, which now lies dead or dying on many open slopes, burnishing the hillsides when the low sun catches them.

In several successive summers a group of travellers settled in a clearing in the wood, with their shawls and babies, guitars and a grey donkey. Smoke was often seen rising from the tree tops, but no one bothered them, and when autumn came they disappeared. Where they went to, or where they go in the summer, remains a mystery but I did come across the remains of their last campsite one day. There was a small pile of ashes and charred wood not far from the little torrent that has its source near the Old Stable; but otherwise they had left the place as they had found it, moss, boulders, trees and all.

At one end of the wood stands a large 17th century farmhouse, grey and tall-chimneyed; it lies half hidden by the encircling trees that seem to have encroached from the wood in the half century since the old family of Watkins moved away. Behind the house are the remains of the original medieval dwelling, roofless now, with its huge chimney breast containing a curving stairway.

In summer and autumn local sheep farmers have always cut down as many bramble thickets in the wood as possible, so that sheep did not become hopelessly tangled in the long suckers when they took shelter from the winter blast. This work has almost ceased so that great banks of thorny stems spread about parts of the wood. I have more than once rescued a sheep in Sylfaen Wood, anchored by its fleece and very hungry. The extra sheepherding needing to prevent this is difficult on farms of ever greater acreage,as one holding takes on adjoining land.

Another steep track leads down from the old farmhouse towards the estuary's edge, passing Cutiau chapel on the way. The tiny congregation worshiped here for the last time in the early 1980s and the slate gravestones see only robins and hedgesparrows now.

It's a far cry from the days when Cutiau was the centre of activity for the district and was packed on Sundays and for treats on special days. Its empty silence contrasts with the day in the Great War when young Hughie Jones and a pal climbed onto the chapel roof when local families were enjoying a special celebration tea in the adjoining schoolroom. The culprits climbed to the top of the roof and placed a large sod on the smoking chimney then withdrew to the hillside bracken to watch the assembled crowd come trooping into the graveyard, clutching handkerchiefs to their faces! The boys were never discovered but certain members of the congregation had their suspicions.

At the far end of Sylfaen Wood stands Moriah Chapel in a wilder, more remote situation at the edge of the coniferous plantations. Moriah was built in the 19th century but its scattered congregation dwindled to nothing fifty years ago and it has been a holiday cottage ever since.

One day, as the afternoon sunlight slanted ever lower through the branches, shedding orange slats across the leaf-strewn forest floor, I went off on a circular walk. As the last light faded between the threatening ragged rain clouds I reached the farmhouse at Llwyn-onn and a roaring fire in the giant hearth. In those last two hours in the valley and through the wood I had seen 14 former farmhouses and cottages - all now derelict or empty for the winter because they are occasional holiday homes.

At the upper edge of Sylfaen Wood stands the humble cottage of Coed-y-foel. Eighty years ago it was the home of William Jones, a likable old bachelor who scraped a living from his tiny tenant holding upon the mountainside. He went to town each Saturday and returned in the afternoon in a merry state. It was his habit to call upon the Joneses at Llwyn-onn and take a cup of tea in order to sober up before traversing the rough ground separating him from his home. He was the last permanent resident of Coed-y-foel; the tiny cottage stood empty for many years, its window frames rotten and the wind off the hills sighing in the stunted oaks and jagged hawthorn nearby.

The great boulder between the house and earth closet is still there, its top split by frost aeons ago. Up here the loud mewing of hunting buzzards is regular music to the ears, a call that William Jones must have known well - like countless generations of hill farmers before him. Today it is a restored holiday home; some of the spirit of the old days has drifted away with the scores of families that have left these high sides of the Mawddach.

Hughie Jones died on Bonfire Night, 1981 and Aunt Mary moved to more congenial surroundings in Barmouth three years later. She died suddenly in May, 1987. They lie in the sunlit graveyard at Llanaber, looking over Cardigan Bay towards the sunset and the far outline of the Llyn hills.

No dairy herd produces milk and butter in the hills above the Mawddach these days. The flocks remain but many of the old families have gone.

3. Major Port of Meirionnydd – The growth and decline of a commercial port

Low tide at the mouth of the Mawddach

E. Hector Kyme

In the years between 1550 and 1603 Barmouth (then called "Abermowe") had only four houses, with two boats based there. At this time it seems the Mawddach entered Cardigan Bay further north than now. Evidence exists to show that the river flowed at the foot of the steep ground to enter the sea where the railway station now stands. Boats entered the harbour between the mainland and Ynys y Brawd but in the early nineteenth century the river began to change its course and eventually entered the sea south of this islet.

From Tudor times to the nineteenth century Barmouth's principal trade was the export of "webs" , a coarse woollen cloth, made in Barmouth and Dolgellau. A century ago one writer put it thus: "Nearly every poor man within these two towns and almost every petty farmer in their vicinity had his loom, wherein he made his webs to support himself and his family".

In the late eighteenth century Dolgellau alone manufactured between £50,000 and £100,000 worth of these webs each year, most of it going to clothe the army. At a time when road transport was insignificant it was easier to export by sea than by land across the wild uplands of the hinterland.

In May, 1797 an Act of Parliament was passed enabling the "repairing, deepening, enlarging and preserving the Harbour of Barmouth in the County of Merioneth". Trustees were appointed "for putting this Act in execution". Soon afterwards these Trustees set about improving the harbour (at that time set further east at the inlet below Orielton woods called Aberamffra Harbour and still a sheltered mooring). They erected a small stone embankment at a cost of £1,660, thus greatly increasing the depth of water. Five years later a completely new quay was constructed.

By 1880 Barmouth had become the most important sea port of Meirionnydd. Even in 1779 Thomas Pennant was able to comment that "this is the port of the county, but not so much frequented as it ought to be, by reason the inhabitants do not attempt commerce on a large scale, but vend their manufactures through the means of factors. Yet ships now and then come and fetch the webs or flannels; and I am informed that a few years ago £40,000 worth have been exported in a year, and £10,000 worth of stockings. Many of the webs are sold into Spain and from thence sent to South America".

A glance at a list of some of the goods imported by sea illustrates how brisk was Barmouth's trade at this time. Vessels known as "coasting vessels" brought coal, wood, slate, ore and corn, alum, alabaster, cheese, flax, bricks, butter, malt, gunpowder, wrought and pig iron, wine, rum, brandy, skins, tallow, pitch, tea, tobacco, flour and lead. The vessels had to pay a duty "not exceeding 3d per ton on all goods excepting coal, limestone, sand and manure for which they were required to pay 2d per ton".

Shipbuilding became an important ancillary industry along the Mawddach. Around 1780 there were three shipbuilding yards at Barmouth and vessels of considerable size were built at Penmaenpool, almost six miles upstream. Even a further mile upstream, at Maes-y-Garnedd, close to Llanelltyd, boats were being built where now the river meanders are narrow and high tides barely cover the infilled marshland.

The launching of a new vessel was often the occasion for celebrating. One especially important day in the history of the town was 8th August, 1838 when two large schooners were launched. One was christened "Ann and Elizabeth" and the other "Maria and Ellen" and after the launching a banquet "was graced by the presence of Sir Watkin Williams Wynne and Sir Robert Williams Vaughan", both members of local aristocratic families."The events of this happy day were duly commemorated by the Bardd Tecwyn and the Bardd Mawddach".

It is hard to imagine the shipbuilding activity that went on in several Mawddach inlets at this time. At Cutiau, two miles along the Dolgella road east of Barmouth, the mouth of the Dwynant was a busy shipyard for many years. Now deposition has allowed the development of extensive marsh with reed beds so that no vessels can approach within hundreds of metres these days. Why should such shipbuilding have been carried on up-river when better facilities were available at Barmouth? It was mainly to relieve the congestion in the town's yards. Shipbuilding flourished to such an extent at one period around Cardigan Bay that it became necessary to use every available creek on the Mawddach. All these new vessels were built using oak grown in the valley so availability of suitable timber near at hand dictated the selection of these creeks.

Such busy shipping activity meant that vessels regularly got into difficulties in the sea off Barmouth. Various attempts were made through the years to erect a lighthouse on Ynys y Brawd. In 1839, for instance, a large four-sided block was begun and erected to twenty feet above high water mark. One night a great storm flattened it so the harbour authorities proposed a round tower on a square base and this was started in 1843. No sooner had it reached the fifteen feet level than a second storm razed it to its foundations and remains as the conspicuous marker of the hazard called Y Perch, out towards the lurking shallows of The Bar.

Up to 1820 a lot of the seaborne trade at Barmouth had been with Ireland, France, Spain and the Americas but after that

Cutiau Chapel today.

There were other causes of shipbuilding's demise, though. It was discovered that the oak of the Mawddach woods developed dry rot. An old tradition states that oak never flourishes near the sea "because the sharp winds cramp the young wood". The advantage of convenient timber supplies quickly turned the isolated creeks into abandoned sites when this problem was discovered.

Sometimes there was another specific reason for a former busy shipyard closing. Such was the case at Cutiau, at the mouth of the Afron Dwynant a couple of miles east of Barmouth on the Dolgellau road. When the Dolgellau - Barmouth highway was re-aligned alongside the shore a stone bridge built over the Afon Dwynant blocked off the creek from the Mawddach estuary. This prevented any further shipbuilding and also meant the owner of Glan-dwr corn mill and farmers having to load and unload their corn that came by sea onto the banking alongside the road. The owner of the banking challenged this and issued legal proceedings against the locals. The latter employed a London barrister to fight their case.

The owner of the land was so enraged that he gave notice to quit to all his cottage tenants and it wasn't long before all the dwellings became vacant. Cutiau Independent Chapel once had more than one hundred members, soon after this only a handful were left and the congregation never really increased again. Certainly this acrimonious affair put a permanent stop to all shipbuilding in this particular Mawddach creek.

Old photographs of the 1880s and 1890s show fishermen still busy at the harbour. There was a thriving herring fishery which continued into the twentieth century. Some commercial fishing existed until after World War Two, but was only slight and sporadic.

Alongside the demise of Barmouth as a commercial port there was the compensation of increasing tourism. The arrival of the railway may have dealt the trade a lethal blow but it was the starting signal for different activities which continue to this day.

date it became increasingly coastal, largely the transporting of timber for the expanding collieries in south Wales, manganese from nearby mines, slates from the small local quarries, and the coarse woollen cloth called "webs". There was still a busy inward trade of corn, flour, coal and the like, a trade which continued until the coming of the railway.

That arrival of the Cambrian Railway in 1867 (see chapter 5) did sound the death knell of Barmouth's importance as a commercial port for Meirionnydd. This decline is highlighted when we read that 169 ships entered Barmouth harbour in 1867 and by 1874 the number was down to 10. Shipping activity, including shipbuilding on the banks of the Mawddach estuary, steadily declined and by 1908 the only large vessel visiting the town was the steamer "Dora", which plied weekly between Liverpool and Barmouth to bring bulky goods and durable foodstuffs.

4. Buried Treasure
Gold mining above the Mawddach

Old gold mine drift above Bontddu.

But the fact that the wedding rings of Queen Mary, wife of George V, and of Princess Marina, Duchess of Kent and the other members of the Royal family were made of Meirionnydd gold few would be aware that this precious metal is found in the wild country of the Mawddach valley.

Fable has it that the Romans were the pioneers of gold mining in Wales but there is no evidence to support this According to available records gold was first discovered in Meirionnydd in 1834 but because such a suggestion was widely ridiculed no mining was done until 1847.

The gold occurs in the Clogau shales of mid-Cambrian strata. The belt where it can be traced runs from a point near Barmouth, heads north then east, immediately to the north of Bontddu.

At one time there was 24 mines in operation but some of the smaller ones never produced any worthwhile return. Only two really managed appreciable results-at the Clogau mine above Bontddu and the Gwynfynydd mine far up the Mawddach valley, well above the head of the estuary.

At the Colgau mine a vein of gold was struck in 1860 and 5 years later the mine paid £22,575 in dividends and in just over three years had produced £43,783-worth of gold. The discovery of gold here at Clogau (sometimes called Saint David's mine) initiated a typical "gold rush" of the sort we associate more with the Klondike than Snowdonia! Many companies sprang up and even before prospecting had been completed costly machinery and buildings were erected. The Mawddach hummed with life and excitement at this time, though many undertakings proved abortive.

Hundreds of men were set to work in the dangerous conditions underground, trekking across the hills from their poverty-stricken farms in the hope of discovering a fortune. Much of the wages they earned were spent in Dolgellu, enriching many local tradesmen. Most of these workers lodged in the barracks set up near the mine and walked home each weekend.

In 1891 four Barmouth business people formed the Clogau Gold Mining Company and in the following 5 years 5,352 ounces of gold were extracted, valued at £19,688. In 1899 this mine was purchased along with other workings in the district and a new company called Saint David's Gold and Copper Mines was formed. During the following few years about 100 miners were employed in the Bontddu district but after the initial impetus of good returns there followed a leaner period of only sporadic discoveries and in 1910 Clogau mine was closed.

The Gwynfynydd mine was originally opened as a lead mine far up the Mawddach valley near Rhaeadr Mawddach (Mawddach Falls). The first gold was discovered here in 1864 and subsequent mining operations were somewhat disjointed - £35,000-worth was produced between 1888 and 1890 and thereafter very little was brought out. The mine was closed in 1916 when most miners were called up for service in the Great War.

The gold mined at Clogau was much finer grain than that from Gwynfynydd but the latter was much lighter in colour because it contained more silver.

But that wasn't the end of the story. In October, 1930 an enquiry opened at Dolgellau under the chairmanship of Professor Louis. It was charged with "the possibilities of developing the production of gold and other materials in Merionethshire". This was the outcome of agitation by several interests urging the government to make a grant towards the re-opening of the gold mines in order to reduce unemployment, then a very serious problem in this part of Wales.

Figures for 1904 were used to justify re-opening - almost 18,500 ounces produced (at £3.16.6(£3.82.5) per ounce) and 500 men employed. However, the enquiry concluded that though there were still unexplored gold veins their number and quality wasn't certain. More money might be spent in searching than would be returned by a discovery - "Mining in this district must be a highly venturesome business".

Since World War Two there has been several attempts to extract gold in various places. In the late fifties, for instance, a local farmer invested capital in a scheme to re-open a Bontddu mine but it was a short-lived enterprise. In the late sixties great consternation was caused when RTZ proposed drilling for gold and copper in the upper Mawddach valley, within what was by that time the Snowdonia National Park.

Even more worrying was a plan by RTZ to dredge the sediments of the actual Mawddach estuary in a bid to extract the alluvial gold deposited there over thousands of years. One scheme associated with this dredging operation would have been the construction of a gravel barrage to block the estuary mouth near the railway bridge; an alternative was to have a huge dredger moving from site to site to dig lagoons within the estuary. Such dredging would have taken 15 years and the massive damage done to this magnificent natural environment is easy to imagine.

It was a great relief to learn in Mach, 1972 that RTZ had abandoned all exploratory drilling in the estuary, "very largely on ecological grounds". Since that time there have been sporadic attempts to extract further gold from old workings, including placer mining (panning) of waste heaps at Gwynfynydd. An enterprising gold mining centre was set up at Dolgellau as a tourist attraction but due to lack of support by the local authorities it was abandoned in the late 1990's.

Such is the nature of gold mining - whether in western Canada or wildest Wales - a highly speculative undertaking! It seems that here in the Mawddach valley the most rewarding days ended with the start of the Great War.

5. Growing Town
Barmouth becomes a Resort

The major contributor to Barmouth's demise as a commercial seaport and the end of the Mawddach as a shipbuilding centre was at the same time instrumental in kickstarting a new chapter in the district's fortunes.

When Archbishop Baldwin of Canterbury and Ranulph de Glanville led the third Crusade in Wales in AD 1188 the party is recorded as having forded the Mawddach estuary at low tide and moved over the mountains northwards to stay at Llanfair, near Harlech. There was no castle, of course, at Harlech at that date. It it not recorded where the large party forded the wet sands of the Mawddach but it is pretty certain to have been well upstream from the sea, for even today (after eight centuries of further infilling by sediments carried down by the river and up by the sea) it is a dangerous and often impossible undertaking below Bontddu.

For the motorist the beautiful Mawddach still presents an obstacle because there is no road bridge below Penmaenpool, 5 miles as-the-crow-flies up from the sea at Barmouth. Even that

Crossing Barmouth Bridge, February, 1959.

is a toll bridge and was not designed to take the heavy flow of traffic of a present summer's day. The only public road over the estuary is at Llanelltyd, 7 miles from Barmouth. Here is the beautiful Llanelltyd Bridge, now listed as an Ancient Monument and only open to pedestrians.

During the middle of the nineteenth century Barmouth became something of a fashionable watering place and a single track railway was developed to the west coast at Aberdyfi, thence north close by the sea through Tywyn and Llwyngwril to the mouth of the Mawddach. At the same time a line was built from Ruabon and Bala westwards down the Wnion Valley to Dolgellau and so, by the southern shore of the Mawddach, to join the other line at Barmouth Junction (later called Morfa Mawddach) on the marshland flats formed at the estuary's mouth. Through an Act of Parliament permission was granted for the erection of a viaduct to carry the railway across the mouth of the Mawddach to Barmouth and work commenced in 1866, despite loud protests from "local inhabitants and eminent visitors". Wordsworth's "sublime estuary" and Ruskin's "Barmouth the Beautiful" were to be "ruined by this hideous metal contraption, by belching smoke, hissing steam and rattling wheels". It is not recorded whether or not many of the more far-sighted tradespeople and inn keepers joined in the general clamour. There was, however, no great national opposition to the erection of the bridge, as might be expected from various amenity societies of the present day; in fact, by 1909 E. Rosalie Jones wrote in her book "History of Barmouth and Vicinity" that the bridge itself was charming.

The mouth of the Maddach is half a mile wide at the point chosen by the bridge builders and at the southern end, across the shallow sands which are exposed at low tide, are 1,927 feet (587 metres) of timber trestle viaduct formed by 113 spans. Next comes a 118 feet (36 metres) long section comprising two steel hog-back lattice girders with steel-plate flooring connecting the timber trestles to the swing bridge section over the narrow, deep-water channel close to the northern bank.

This swing bridge is supported in the centre on four steel cylinders filled with concrete and with a turntable on top and is 133 feet (40 metres) long. The final, northernmost section consists of two spans of parallel-flanged plate girders and is 75 feet (23 metres) long, supported upon masonry abutment. The whole structure is 751 yards and 6 inches (686 metres) long and besides carrying the single track railway line there is a footbridge on the eastern (upstream) side which is open to the public.

A Railway Act required that the swing bridge be opened to tall vessels going up-river. However, since the coming of the railway to Barmouth few vessels of any size have plied beyond the bridge and the swing section is now rarely opened. On one post-war occasion when it was opened for a yacht race upstream to Penmaenpool the operation took so long that by the time it was opened the vessels couldn't reach their destination as the tide was starting to fall. The bridge's greatest moment of glory, though, was when it was used for dramatic location shots during the filming of the thriller "The Ghost Train".

The coming of the railway and its bridge sounded the death knell to Barmouth as a seaport and the Mawddach as a boat building centre. It was rumoured that the erection of the bridge would cause the Mawddach to fill up with sand. Deposits of mud and sand are certainly filling in creeks and being colonised by marsh plants whose roots anchor the sediments and turn them into dry land.

Ten years after Barmouth Bridge was built it was discovered that in certain places along the banks of the estuary there was a profusion of common scurvy grass, a known cure for certain forms of scurvy. It is recorded that invalids suffering from the ailment "found the application of the herb and a course of baths in the sea efficacious remedies". Even more trains rattled over the bridge and the town flourished, changing from a seaport to a holiday resort.

The line up the south bank of the Mawddach that connected Morfa Mawddach and Dolgellau and on to Corwen and Ruabon was a victim of the notorious "Beeching cuts" in the early sixties. No longer is it possible to watch from my late aunt's farm at Llwyn-onn and see the distant smoke and steam of trains conveying goods and passengers (the majority of them holiday makers bound for the sunny sands beside Cardigan Bay). You could almost set your watch by the sight of the last evening train drifting eastwards towards Dolgellau, a single

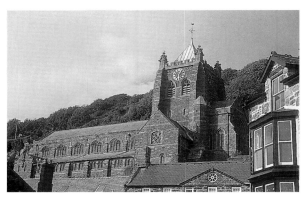

The Church of Saint John the Evangelist, Barmouth.

coach pulled by an antique Great Western "coffee pot" right up to the withdrawal of services.

After the "Beeching cuts" a new threat hung over Barmouth's railway viaduct when it was discovered that the timbers of the trestle section had been attacked by ship's worm below high water mark. Happily a lengthy regime of treatment killed the worm and the expensive repairs were undertaken.

The railway's arrival gave a major impetus to the town's building trade and a "new town" rapidly grew up between the old settlement perched on the crags below Dinas Oleu and the seashore. New places of worship were erected as well as shops and houses, and in 1870 the Cors-y-Gedol was rebuilt as the major hotel.

Most of the new properties were built in the "Victorian Terrace" style, using the hard, grey stone of the district. These long, tall terraces are still an impressive feature of the town, dwellings that served in the majority of cases as boarding houses and hotels for a century and more.

The value of the limited areas of building land soon became very great, as much as £3 per square yard being paid in the late nineteenth century. Water supply was proving a problem as only three main springs served the growing town. About 1880 the local board engaged a firm of civil engineers to design a better supply based on a 89,000 gallons capacity masonry reservoir above Llanaber, two miles north of the town. This was completed in 1884 and a cast iron pipe delivered an unreliable supply to parts of Barmouth. The scheme proved an utter failure because the mountain stream feeding the dam was apt to dry up in dry periods - just when the population was hugely increased by holidaymakers.

The same firm of engineers was engaged by Barmouth town council in 1890 to come up with a better scheme. This time Llyn Bodlyn was brought into play, a natural lake 5 miles (8 kilometres) north of the town in a remote hollow under the west side of Diffwys. With a surface at 1,250 feet (381 metres) above sea level gravity would play a major part in ensuring Barmouth's future supplies. A massive masonry dam raised the water level an extra 10 feet (3 metres) with a surface area of 40 acres (16.6 hectares) and a capacity of 102 million gallons.

The annual rainfall of more than 80 inches (2000mm) in the drainage basin of Llyn Bodlyn has ensured a sufficient supply ever since, though a firm of consultants reported in 1901 that the new scheme was "unsatisfactory". As the demands for water increased through the twentieth century it was necessary to install a booster plant along the main water pipe north of the town and this certainly helped to maintain pressure at busy holiday times.

The spate of building in the last years of the late Victorian era and into the early twentieth century is still well seen today. There is evidence in some of the names given to thoroughfares - Jubilee Road, King George Street and King's Crescent (named in honour of Edward VII). Hotels, houses and shops were built far beyond the needs of the time, representing a progressive outlook on the part of the council and private developers. Most of the stone came from the large quarry cut into the Cambrain strata near the harbour. It hasn't been used for many years and is partly covered by natural vegetation but there have been landslips here in recent years.

One reason why so many of the hotels and private houses built at this time before the Great War look so similar is that people settling here, mainly from the Midlands, were wealthy and could afford the space and style of the houses easily mistaken for hotels.

The town's original parish church is Saint Bodwen's at Llanber; dating from the thirteenth century it is claimed as "the most notable example of early English architecture in north Wales". Saint David's church was built in early Victorian days on the site of a former shipbuilding yard near the harbour as a much more accessible place of worship for townsfolk and visitors.

Optimistic plans to build a much larger church only materialised as a result of generous financial support by Mrs Dyson Perrins of the wealthy family that manufactured Worcestershire Sauce and who lived here at Plas Mynach along the Llanaber Road.. She initially subscribed £15,000, three quarters of the entire anticipated cost. The foundation stone of the new church, Saint John the Evangelist, was laid by the Prince and Princess of Battenberg in 1889.

Built on a ledge of the hillside directly above the town there were ominous rumours that because the ledge was too narrow the building might collapse. These fears were well founded because one Saturday morning in September, 1891 the massive tower being built at the south end of the church suddenly collapsed and fell into the church, demolishing a lot of what had already been erected. All work stopped and it was doubted that the church could ever be completed. Mrs Dyson Perrins, however, came to the rescue and the building was consecrated in November, 1895 by the Bishop of Bangor. In 1909 she endowed a further £10,000 to what is one of the finest parish churches in north Wales

Right through this period of growth Barmouth and its noble natural surroundings were visited by the famous and discerning. Some of these were:

Percy Bysshe Shelley
The poet came to north Wales with his wife and sister-in-law in the spring of 1812. They were looking for a home where he intended "to dwell forever". Having first stayed at Holyhead they arrived at Barmouth three days later but couldn't find anywhere that suited them so embarked in a open boat for Aberystwyth, and on again to Cwm Elan where they eventually settled.

William Wordsworth
During his travels between 1823 and 1825 Wordsworth arrived in Barmouth in 1824 and hired a boat "and rowed up its sublime Estuary, which many compare with the finest in Scotland. With a fine sea view in front, the mountains behind, the glorious Estuary running eight miles inland, and Cader Idris within compass of a day's walk, Barmouth can always hold its own against any rival".

Charles Darwin
The nineteenth century celebrity with the longest association with the area was Charles Darwin. He first came here in the

summer of 1828 when he was a 19 year old Cambridge student and a member of a reading party under a "very dull" private tutor charged with attempting to get some mathematics into his pupils' heads. What Darwin did discover on this trip were "some of the rarest British insects" in and around Barmouth.

He came back in June of the following year, to collect interesting insects. In August, 1831 Darwin accompanied the great pioneer geologist Professor Adam Sedgwick through north Wales. It was Sedgwick that gave the name to the Cambrain geological era. At the end of this tour Darwin left Sedgwick at Capel Curig "and went in a straight line by compass and map across the mountains to Barmouth, never following any track unless it coincided with my course". Once arrived there he joined his Cambridge friends and they took daily walks over the hills behind the town, boated on the Mawddach, sailed to Saint Patrick's Causeway to land at low tide, or fished the Cors-y-Gedol lakes inland from Tal-y-Bont.

At these times Darwin never missed an opportunity to "entomologise most industriously", collecting and preserving insects that seemed worthy of further examination.

Darwin didn't return to Barmouth until he was 60 years old, in 1869. He stayed at the lovely house of Caerdeon, overlooking the northern shore of the Mawddach three miles east of Barmouth with his family and spent time working on various projects, including the manuscript of "The Descent of Man". He wrote from Caerdeon to his mentor Sir Joseph Dalton Hooker, the eminent botanist, that the view was superb - "Old Cader is a grand fellow, and shows himself off superbly with every changing light". Darwin was not well during his stay at Caerdeon, complaining of being "in a very poor way". These later years were plagued with the unknown illness we now know to be Chagas' disease which he picked up during his South American journeys. Though he didn't die until 1882 this was his last visit to the beautiful Barmouth neighbourhood.

Alfred Tennyson
Eleven years after Darwin's first visit to Barmouth Tennyson undertook a tour of north Wales (1839). He thought the town prettier than Aberystwyth and the sandy shore "looking Mablethorpe-like" (he was, after all, a native of Lincolnshire). He loved the Mawddach, "a long estuary with cloud-capped hills running up as far as Dolgellau". Only one of his "In Memorium" poems dwells on Tennyson's sense of joyous peace

Saint George's Cottages, Barmouth.

in the natural world and this was written at Barmouth. It ends thus:

"From belt to belt of crimson seas
On leagues of odour streaming far,
To where in yonder Orient star
A thousand spirits whisper 'Peace'."

John Ruskin
The most famous art critic of nineteenth century Britain was distressed by what he foresaw as the inevitable breakdown of

Cardigan Bay from the "Golden Gate" adjacent to Dinas Oleu, above Barmouth.

order after the fashion of the French Revolution almost a hundred years earlier. He propounded his ideas to save the day in the establishment of "The Guild of Saint George" which would sweep away all social barriers. In a series of letters to "the working men of England" he appealed for co-operation in his scheme.

Before going ahead in a big way he knew it was necessary to experiment and at the end of 1874 Mrs Fanny Talbot (1824 -1917) of Ty' n y Ffynon, highest situated house in the town, made an offer of a dozen cottages and a piece of land adjacent to her home near the top of the old part of Barmouth. Unfortunately Ruskin was far from well at this time and unable to visit the site of his bold experiment until all legal details had transferred the properties into the ownership of the Guild. It's interesting to note some of Ruskin's rules governing these cottages:

(i)   Mrs Talbot is in absolute control of the property.
(ii)   Cottages to be kept at original low rentals.
(iii)   No tenant accepted unless of good character.
(iv)   Rent must be paid punctually.
(v)   Each tenant to be personally known and administered to in sickness.
(vi)   Gifts of warm clothing and coal at Christmas.
(vii)   Gifts of tea and cake to celebrate the Master's (Ruskin's) birthday.

Eventually, in the summer of 1876, Ruskins was able to visit Barmouth. He met the tenants, who included a Ggaribaldi look-alike and thought himself a great scholar but commented that in his opinion Ruskin said some good things but it was a pity he didn't write better English !

23

Another tenant was the exiled French social reformer Auguste Guyard who had attempted to bring about a better way of life for the inhabitants of Frotey-les-Vesoul, his birthplace. But the Catholic church felt threatened and despite close friendship with the likes of Alexander Dumas and Victor Hugo he had to abandon his scheme of life improvement for fellow villagers. With the outbreak of the Franco-Prussian War in 1870 he fled with his daughters to this country, living at No.2, Rock Terrace, Barmouth (a Guild of Saint George cottage) until his death in 1882. His chief delight was the cultivation of his garden and the planting of trees upon the surrounding rock ledges above the town.

He was given permission to be buried at a spot 150 feet (45 metres) above his cottage home, next to Mrs Talbot's boundary wall; and we can still examine what has come to be known as "the Frenchman's Grave" at the top of old Barmouth.

After Ruskin left Barmouth in that summer of 1876 he became ill and never had opportunity to expand his scheme of social reform. Those humble dwellings still stand on the mountainside, looking out over Barmouth's rooftops to Cardigan Bay.

William Gladstone

In September, 1892 the Prime Minister and his wife left Porthmadog by special train to arrive at Barmouth and be presented with a special address offered by the townsfolk. The Gladstones stayed here for a week "to the great delight of the inhabitants". Now aged 82 Gladstone had just became Prime Minister for the fourth time, two years before his final retirement from politics.

The craggy hillside above the old town has an interesting story to tell. One of the pioneer conservation thinkers at the end of the nineteenth century, Canon Rawnsley, had been staying with a friend, Mrs Talbot (that same woman who had donated land and property to The Guild of Saint George) here at Barmouth. As soon as the National Trust had been formed in February, 1895 Mrs Talbot gave 4.5 acres (1.9 hectares) of land above Idris Lane and Saint George's Lane; it is called Dinas Oleu and has the distinction of being the very first land acquired by the National Trust. A further 12 acres (5 hectares) adjoining Dinas Oleu, called Cae Fadog, was bought in 1980 to add to this historic territory.

Some measure of the district's growing popularity and accessibility after the railway arrived can be understood when we realise the number of artists - mainly from the Midlands - that visited and worked around the Mawddach. The Mawddach Valley became as popular with the artists as Beddgelert, Betws-y-coed and Capel Curig further to the north. Some of the best known who regularly painted in the district are members of the famous Williams family - Sidney Richard Percy (1821 - 86) was fifth son of Edward Williams Snr. and became a very popular landscape painter, as did his brother Henry John Boddington (1811 - 65). Both of them changed their names to avoid confusion with other members of this artistic family. Then there was Walter Williams (1836 - 1906), William Henry Mander, Alfred de Breanski Snr. and William Mellor among many professionals drawn to paint the Mawddach and surrounding hills in all their many moods. When their works come on the market these days they command high prices.

That the town itself had become a popular, bustling resort each summer season is evidenced by noting that General Booth of the Salvation Army addressed a great crowd in the Assembly Rooms in August, 1907; in the first years of the twentieth century performances by Miss Marie Hall, tenor John McCormick and Beethoven interpreter Wilhelm Backhaus "have all delighted summer audiences at Barmouth".

6. Sunny Sands – Barmouth in the Twentieth Century

Above Hendremynach in 1929. The Promenade had not yet been built as the author's mother looks down to Plas Mynach (left in the trees) and Ty Graig.

This story is about holidays on the Cardigan Bay coast and because I've known the Barmouth district all my life (and my parents knew it before I was born) it is something of a personal memoir.

After my parents' marriage on Midsummer's Day, 1929 they planned a honeymoon on the Devon coast and to take along my mother's unmarried sister - my Aunt Mary - too. By the time they had reached the West Midlands their car was showing signs of unreliability. A change of plans was indicated. A work colleague of my father had recently returned from a holiday on the Welsh coast at Barmouth and extolled the virtues of the area. Without further ado my parents changed direction, heading west to the coast of Cardigan Bay.

The journey wasn't without incident. On the steep climb between Dinas Mawddwy and Dolgellau the clutch slipped so badly that my mother and Aunt Mary had to run behind the car carrying rocks which they jammed behind the wheels whenever the car ran out of forward momentum. They eventually arrived at Dolgellau and stayed the night there before completing the last ten miles to Barmouth next day.

The Mount Argus Hotel, perched beside the steep hill road leading up towards the Panorama Walk, became their base for annual holidays most summers though the thirties. The proprietors were Mrs Barnard and her daughter, Bess, who are still remembered by older Barmouth residents.

Looking through family photograph albums of the time we see tennis parties, picnics in the hills of the Harlech Dome, bucket-and-spade days on the beach, sailing in Cardigan Bay. It was considered de riguer for able-bodied parties to make at least one expedition on foot from Barmouth to the top of Cadair Idris and back, via Barmouth Bridge, each holiday; there are several photographs of my mother near the summit on what always seem to be grey, misty days.

A particularly sharp memory is of the day when I was promised a great treat. After lunch we sat in a high window at Mount Argus Hotel and I was told to look out for something special. The joy in my heart cannot be described as a pony was led into view. It was to be mine for the afternoon; we were to trek up the narrow road to Llwyn- onn and beyond. I was supremely happy, and I have photographs to prove it!

One summer before I was born my parents rented an Edwardian "cottage" high above the Llanaber road a mile north of Barmouth. Photographs show my mother sitting in a drawing room in the still-brilliant light of a late June evening - it was still light at eleven o' clock at midsummer on this west coast. Photographs also show the sea front before the construction of the sea defence works – the so-called Promenade. Before 1930 the low ground at the northern end of the town was regularly flooded when the high tides coincided with strong west or south-west winds. The entire west front of Barmouth was situated on the edge of unstable dunes and beach; many hotels and boarding houses were threatened with subsidence.

In 1930 Barmouth council obtained a loan of £85,000 to build a sea wall. Work began that year to construct a 1.3 mile (2.1 km) promenade that consisted of a sloping apron and steps with a walkway and wide road on the inland side. Timber groins were erected below the apron, about 40 yards apart.

In the spring of 1931 a powerful storm broke through the unfinished promenade in two places - near Marine Mansions and opposite the Min-y-Mor Hotel. A second loan had to be obtained to do the repairs, bringing the total borrowings to £110,000. Such was the crippling effect on the council finances that for decades the development of the other amenities in the town was curtailed. In 1956 it was found that a quarter of a century of erosion had damaged the front of the

The damaged Promenade in August, 1931, looking south to Min-y-Mor Hotel.

27

apron and a new concrete and steel footing had to be built. Though crippling for the town's civic finances the promenade has been a great asset in allowing development of the land behind it. The appeal of Barmouth as a holiday resort was enhanced, too, making much more of the fine, sandy beach accessible.

After the Great War the Fairbourne Miniature Railway was built along the length of Ro Wen, almost to the end of the spit on the south side of the Mawddach's mouth opposite Barmouth. In the summer season boatmen run a pedestrian ferry service from the town's harbour to the beach on Ro Wen's tip to connect with these miniature train trips of almost two miles across the dunes to Fairbourne village.

During the early thirties my parents hired the yacht "Surprise" for long sailing trips in Cardigan Bay and out into the Irish Sea, including explorations of the Saint Tudwal's Islands off

"Surprise" in Barmouth harbour, 1932.
Below: The author's mother mackerel fishing on board "Surprise", 1933.

John Ellis Morris on "Surprise" in the Irish Sea.

the south coast of the Llyn peninsula. At a later time I, too, joined them, in a Moses basket lashed to the deck.

In the summer of 1933 the country was agog with news of the Loch Ness "monster" in the Scottish Highlands. A circus owner offered £20,000 to anyone who could capture it alive and deliver it to him. No-one managed to claim the prize but my father rigged up a set of old car tyres and, helped by John Morris and his son Willie, they towed the "monster" up and down the Mawddach behind "Surprise". Onlookers on the shore were deceived and waved frantically to the sailors, believing them to be in mortal danger !

The Mawddach "monster" near the mouth of the estury in the summer of 1933.

Post-war heatwave on Barmouth beach. Left to right: The author's mother, the author, Aunt Mary (behind) and Mary Savage.

World War Two was a quiet time in the district, as for most remote rural areas of Britain. Holidaymakers virtually ceased, though military camps here and there in Meirionnydd brought some trade to local businesses. With the return of peace some things changed forever.

My parents were unable to sail the "Surprise" again and Mrs Barnard and Bess had left the Mount Angus Hotel. One interesting incident involving Bess Barnard immediately prior to the start of the war concerned a famous photographer. One day she met a tall, middle aged man on the hillside above Barmouth. He asked her if she could direct him to the Panorama Walk. Ever an enthusiast she said she would take him there as it was only half a mile away. To her surprise she soon discovered that her companion was no other than W.A (Walt) Poucher, the famous mountain photographer, and that

Summer afternoon at the northern end of Barmouth promenade in post-war days. The author's mother (back row, third left), Millie Morris (back row, fourth left), the author's father (standing, right), the author (front row, second left).

he was taking photographs for a new book about Wales. That book was eventually published after the war as "Wandering in Wales", a book I regularly borrowed as a child from the local library; to me it was a sort of Bible and the photograph of Barmouth's Panorama over the Mawddach to Cadair Idris was a favourite - but I didn't hear of the connection with Bess Barnard until many years later.

We resumed our annual holidays at Barmouth in the memorably hot, dry summer of 1947. Our neighbours at home in Derbyshire had earlier in the year taken tenancy of Peny-Gribin. This was a delightful, former gamekeeper's cottage on the steep hillside above Bontddu, five miles upstream of Barmouth with fantastic views across the estuary to the foothills and ramparts of Cadair Idris. They used it as a second home for several years in the late forties.

We were now based each holiday at the Victoria Hotel overlooking Barmouth's Promenade and well remembered for its wonderful catering by all who stayed with Mrs Brown and her daughter. But the days of the town as a traditional resort were already numbered. As car ownership spread and overseas holidays became the norm long-stay visitors gave way to day trippers and a huge tide of caravan sites spread across the sandy flats to the north, at Tal-y-bont and Dyffryn Ardudwy. The larger hotels closed as demand fell away, summer traffic caused ever greater traffic congestion through a town with no space for a by-pass.

Standing on the Promenade on a sunlit summer's evening you could look south to the hillside above Arthog, across the mouth of the Mawddach, and make out the outline of the famous "monk" in the abandoned slate quarry high above the coast. He no longer looks out towards Barmouth because the quarry trees have grown these last fifty years to hide him. The memory of him, though, reminds those who knew him of happy days by the sea in times long gone.

7. For Those In Peril On The Sea.
The RNLI at Barmouth

The "Jones Gibb II" returning to Barmouth harbour in rough weather in 1932. This was Barmouth's last lifeboat equipped with sails.

It was natural that Barmouth, as a leading Cardigan Bay port, should be involved with sea rescue from an early date. It wasn't long after the founding of the Royal National Lifeboat Institution in the spring of 1824 that a group of Barmouth residents requested that a lifeboat be stationed here.

The Board of Trade Shipwreck Maritime Board agreed to supply a 26 feet Palmer vessel, propelled by six oars and costing £56. It came into service in 1828 and Barmouth has had a lifeboat ever since.

That original, nameless lifeboat was instrumental in saving 100 lives in the years up to 1850, when she became unfit for service and a new, self-righting boat propelled by eight oars replaced her. This was the first boat at this station supplied by the RNLI.

After saving 56 lives in the next 13 years this second lifeboat was replaced in January, 1867 by the "Ellen" (probably the Christian name of the anonymous woman who provided the necessary £300). By 1885 the vessel was in need of replacement and the wealthy Mrs Jones-Gibb of Tunbridge Wells, Kent came to the rescue with the £390 required to build the new vessel which, at 12 oars double-banked had two more than the "Ellen". The new boat was named the "Jones-Gibb" and the donor also paid for the cost of a new slipway to make launching easier.

It's easy to see that Barmouth's importance as a commercial port waned steadily through the second half of the nineteenth century by noting that in the 13 years' service of the second lifeboat (1853 - 1866) 15 launches saved 56 lives whereas in the 20 years' service of the "Jones-Gibb" (1885 - 1905) 19 launches saved 22 lives. Coastal commercial shipping in Cardigan Bay was certainly curtailed after the coming of the railway in 1867.

Mrs Jones-Gibb (by now re-married as Mrs G.G.Smart) came to the rescue again in 1904 and paid the cost of £1,032 for a new, more up-to-date replacement, also named "Jones-Gibb". The Barmouth crew chose a 38 feet non-self-righting, rowing and sailing model. George Lennox Watson was the RNLI's Consulting Naval Architect and had an international reputation and subsequently became famous as the designer of the Royal Yacht "Britannia" and large yachts contesting the America's Cup.

At this period there was a feeling that self-righting meant instability and some crews of smaller lifeboats described them as "roly-polies". Watson suggested that the smaller pulling lifeboats should remain self-righting but that larger sailing-and-pulling boats, like this new "Jones-Gibb", would be better for crews if they were not self-righting.

Barmouth's new "Jones-Gibb" came into service at New Year, 1905. This was the station's last sailing-and-pulling boat and was based here until the outbreak of World War Two. Family photographs show this fine lifeboat entering Barmouth harbour under sail in foul weather, returning after a rescue in 1932.

At the outbreak of World War Two Barmouth got its first motor lifeboat. This "Surf" class vessel cost almost £3,500 and was paid for by the wealthy Mrs. M. A. Ardern of Pretsbury, Cheshire and was named " Lawrence Ardern, Stockport" in a quayside ceremony performed by Lady Harlech. Most of this lifeboat's war time rescues involved crashed aircraft. It served for ten years and was replaced by "The Chieftain", a larger "Liverpool" class boat in 1949. After 33 years it in turn was replaced by the 'Rother' class boat "Princess of Wales" and ten years later, in 1992, this too was replaced by the "Mersey" class boat "Moira Barrie" which these days lies at anchor as the station's offshore lifeboat, too large to be housed in the building and its slipway adjoining the railway viaduct.

In 1967 " The Chieftain" was joined by Barmouth's first inflatable inshore lifeboat. Today there is a D class I.L.B. on station.

As in so many places around the British coast lifeboats have tended to be crewed by particular families; a sort of heredity of service. One such at Barmouth was the Morris family. John Morris was the coxswain of both the first and second "Jones-Gibb" boats from 1892 to 1922. His eldest son was John Ellis Morris, (see page 28) a crew member for more than 46 years and coxswain of the second "Jones-Gibb" and "Lawrence Ardern, Stockport" between 1930 and 1947. He was Harbour Master for twenty years (1934-54). His brother O. Tom Morris was a crew member for 44 years and his brother, Fan Morris, crewed the lifeboat for a similar length of time.

John Ellis Morris's son, William ("Willie"), joined the crew of the second "Jones-Gibb" in 1925 aged seventeen. He served as mechanic under his father in the "Lawrence Ardern, Stockport" and then as mechanic on "The Chieftain". He is

On board a visiting warship at the mouth of the Mawddach in the fifties. Left to right: Willie Morris, the author's mother, Millie Morris, Marian Williams, naval officer, Beryl Morris, the author (in front).

well remembered locally as the recipient of the Maud Smith Award for the bravest act of life saving by a lifeboat crew member in 1957. "Willie" put to sea in his own motor launch "The Skylark" and rescued four swimmers who were in difficulties off Barmouth beach in July, 1957. It was the first time the Maud Smith Award had been made for a rescue carried out by a lifeboat crew member using his own boat. This illustrious award was presented to "Willie" Morris by Princes Marina, Duchess of Kent at Central Hall, Westminster.

"Willie" finally retired in March, 1970 after 45 years as a lifeboatman. He died in 1996 aged 88.

The lifeboat house beside Barmouth railway viaduct has long been too small to contain modern vessels, which have lain at anchor in the harbour. A new sophisticated lifeboat station on the sea front north of the harbour opened in 2004. It houses the offshore lifeboat, the 12 metre "Mersey" class "Moira Barrie", and the D class inshore boat on respective trailers. The original plan to build a new station with slipway on the "island" at the northern mouth of the Mawddach (now connected to the promenade by a road) was refused by the planning authorities on environmental grounds.

The new station also contains a shop, viewing platform and museum but many believe that launching will be comparatively slow, involving time-consuming journeys on tractor-hauled trailers.

Whatever people's opinion of the new scheme, the town's long association with the rescue of those in peril on the sea will continue towards and beyond this station's bicentenary.

8. Cadair Idris – Queen of Eryri

The north face of Cadair Idris from near Llwyn-onn, July afternoon.

Once upon a time there were local residents who should have known better when they claimed that Cadair Idris has the second highest summit in Wales! It is actually the eighteenth highest, failing to reach the magic 3,000 feet (914 metres) by 70 feet (21 metres).

It may not be in the top altitude league of Welsh peaks but it can lay claim to being the most beautiful. Actually I think the northern side of the mountain can claim to be second in the beauty stakes, after the Snowdon group. But it's all a matter of personal preference.

Certainly no Welsh mountain massif has the same bold east - west watershed, casting down great rock exposures to the north and south and clasping beautiful little lakes in the embrace of supporting ridges. When seen from the southern slopes of the Harlech Dome on a sunlit evening the huge north faces come alive, each gully etched with black shadow, each falling arête highlighted by the low angled light. One disadvantage of the mountain's position so close to the coast is that a good covering of snow and ice is fairly rare. No sooner has Cadair Idris doubled its apparent stature after snowfall than it dissipates, though Diffwys and the distant Arans continue to emulate Alpine giants.

Beginning in the eighteenth century this physical beauty wasn't lost on celebrated artists. Richard Wilson (1714-82), perhaps the greatest of all Welsh artists, came to appreciate his native landscape more acutely after years in Italy and London. Two of his most celebrated works are "Snowdon" (done about 1770 showing the west side of the mountain rising above the Nantlle valley) and "Cadair Idris' (showing the mountain and Cwm Cau and now in the Tate Gallery).

Clearly visible from Barmouth harbour in fine weather Cadair Idris has always been more popular with mountain walkers than the heights of the Harlach Dome just behind the town. It used to be the done thing for walkers to reach the top of Cadair Idris by way of Barmouth Bridge, Arthog and so up to Llynau Cregennen before climbing to the watershed and traversing behind Tyrau Mawr to reach the summit of Pen-y-Gadair, the mountain's highest top. These days fewer people bother to do what is a grand, varied round;

The path to Cadair Idris. The author's mother (left) and Aunt Mary on the hills above Arthog, 1930.

most park a car near Llyn Gwernan and go straight up the short, steep Fox's Path to the top.

My parents used to do the long circuit of Barmouth, Arthog, Pen-y-Gadair, Fox's Path and back across Barmouth Bridge - a round of at least 17 miles (27 kms). The present refuge on

The author's mother on the summit of Cadair Idris, June, 1930.

kettle was singing over the flames and topped up his cup whereupon the old girl reappeared to announce in broken English "that will be another ten pence-we have to carry up every drop of water from Dolgellau!" Having reluctantly paid the extra charge the party set off down towards the top of the Fox's Path. Imagine their surprise on finding a lad from the summit tearoom filling a bucket at a clear spring only a stone's throw below the summit!

Cadair Idris was a popular mountain to climb even in the earliest nineteenth century. It was possible to hire a guide for 6 shillings (30p) and a pony for 8 shillings (40p). In the 1860's a Dolgellau guide called Pugh climbed to the top four times in a single day to win a wager of £10 from a group of Cambridge visitors!

A well remembered day associated with this mountain concerns a planned circuit to traverse the Harlech Dome foothills eastward past Bontddu, cross the Mawddach by the toll bridge at Penmaenpool and climb the wooded valley behind to go up by the Fox's Path to the summit. Then we were to traverse Pen-y-Gadair westwards to Tyrau Mawr and so down to Arthog and over Barmouth Bridge. It was going to be a long day and the weather forecast was not good.

It was August, 1979 and as we crossed the woods behind Bontddu the summits of Cadair Idris disappeared into gathering cloud, then as we crossed the toll bridge to Penmaenpool the wind strengthened. The first spots of rain fell as we climbed the wooded valley above King's Youth Hostel, going up through the area called Islawr-dref.

It was now raining hard and the wind speed increased all the time. We decided it was unwise to go up onto the mountain, particularly as visibility would be nil and we'd be soaked in a matter of minutes. As things turned out it was the right decision.

Walking along the old Dolgellau-Tywyn road towards Llynau Cregennen we now faced hurricane winds and driving rain. It was cold and very unpleasant-but not as unpleasant as the conditions being faced by competitors in the Fastnet yacht race. Looking back it wasn't really

the 2,930 feet (893 metres)summit replaces what was in pre-war days a hovel where refreshments were served to walkers. On one of the occasions that my parents reached the summit, in the early thirties, they were served cups of tea and the old lady withdrew to the back room. Having drunk half of his tea my father went over to the fire where a black surprising to learn that 23 boats were sunk or abandoned and 15 lives lost.

There were times as we went along when there was no choice but to crouch behind a sheltering wall as a particulaly vicious blast threw a wall of water at us. Wind speed must have exceeded 100 mph; we had made a very wise decision to bypass the summit ridge. By the time we got down to Barmouth Bridge wind speeds had lessened but we still had to claw our way across with tall, white horses tossing spray right over our heads.

9. Hills of the Harlech Dome

Diffwys (2,461 feet) from Craig-y-Grit on the Llawlech ridge, autumn afternoon.

Diffwys (left) and Y Garn from Llwyn-onn on a summer afternoon in 1973.

The great swathe of high land inland from Barmouth and north of the Mawddach estuary is still a district of unknown hollows and green heights. A long, curving arc of high ground - the main watershed - sweeps from the back of Barmouth right up to overlook the Vale of Ffestiniog.

The two Rhinogs - Fawr and Fach - may present the roughest, toughest going of any of the hills in Britain but they are not as high as Y Llethr and Diffwys, nearer the Mawddach.

Rhinog Fawr (2,362 feet/720 metres) and Rhinog Fach (2,336 feet/712 metres) are really too far away to concern us here; suffice to say that the old trackway crossing the ridge just north of Rhinog Fawr at Bwlch Tyddiad and called the Roman Steps is probably medieval and its lovely, flagged surface may well date from that time, not Roman times.

The highest summit of the Harlech Dome is Y Llethr- " the slope"-at 2,480 feet (756 metres) and from it a fairly sharp ridge runs south to lead up to the top of Diffwys - "the precipice" - at 2,461 feet (750 metres). This is the only high top of the Harlech Dome visible from the slopes above the Mawddach, an enchanting focal point in some atmospheric conditions, leading the eye up to the sky when seen from the country above Cutiau, Llwyn-onn and Bontddu.

This high ground behind Barmouth has never featured in the first rank of mountain activity; it never seems to have drawn quantities of pioneering mountaineers through the years. One reference to the lofty ridge between Diffwys and Y Llethr relates to an account by Geoffrey Winthrop Young and a companion going up beside the long wall, towards the top of Y Llethr, on a misty day before the outbreak of the Great War.

Pont Fadog over the Afon Ysgethin near Cors-y-gedol.

Then there was the sad case of a youth climbing in search of raven's eggs on Craig Bodlyn, on the shadowy northern flank of Diffwys. He fell and was killed, the forlorn spot marked by a memorial tablet.

The hill wanderer exploring these grassy ridges in the years after World War Two may have well met the wiry presence of Major Bill Tilman, probably the finest mountain explorer of the twentieth century who in later years took to sailing to his mountains - to places like Patagonia and to the Southern Ocean. Tilman lived with his sister at Bod Owen, a Regency house overlooking the Mawddach estuary a couple of miles east of Barmouth. He was a regular visitor of Hughie Jones and Aunt Mary, calling in at Llwyn-onn while walking the hills with his beloved dogs. He disappeared without trace alongside the rest of the crew of an old sailing boat in the south Atlantic in 1978, aged 80.

I can recommend no better route on this southern part of the Harlech Dome than to climb up through Barmouth old town, past that pioneer National Trust plot of Dinas Oleu and through the so-called "Golden Gate" and so up the rugged ground of Garn Gorllwyn and across the pass of Bwlch y Llan. Keeping to the ridge-top there are ever broader vistas out over Cardigan Bay to the south coast of the

The old inn at Bwlch-y-Goedloedd, near the Panorama Walk, above Barmouth.

Y Garn and the Dwynant Valley from above Llwyn-onn Isaf.

Llyn peninsula, away towards the north-west. The ground mounts steadily up, over Sylfaen Mountain to come to the next pass - Bwlch y Rhiwgyr - from where there is a good prospect down to the north, over the land of Ardudwy.

This ancient land may be built of very hard rocks but it is not as solid as maybe expected. The whole of north-western Wales is periodically subject to earth tremors. In July, 1984 an earthquake centred on the Llyn peninsula had a magnitude of 5.4 on the Richter scale and movements were felt in the Barmouth area. Aunt Mary was walking her dog on the beach when the ground shook so violently that she thought she had become dizzy! It was Britain's strongest on-shore shock of the twentieth century.

Beyond Bwlch y Rhiwgyr we can follow the broad, grassy ridge-top onwards towards Diffwys. This next long section

is Llawlech and halfway to the summit it is crossed by the old trackway that was once the main link between Llanbedr and Bontddu. This was the route used by the gold miners and other travellers from Harlech Castle towards England. The highest point of the track over the watershed is Bwlch Llawlech (1,825 feet/ 556 metres) and even today it is easy to imagine old timers traversing this lonely country to and from the Mawddach's shore.

The long wall that leads all the way to the summit of Diffwys is a useful guide in poor visibility; it is said to have been built by French prisoners during the Napoleonic wars. Nearer our own time Major Tilman and friends hauled fuel to the top of Diffwys for a celebration bonfire on Coronation night, 1953 but few saw it blazing from afar because of clinging mist!

From the top a good walk back, to complete a circuit, is to follow the south ridge over Craig Aderyn and so by descending into Cwm Hirgwm either go down to Bontddu on the Barmouth - Dolgellau road or turn up to the west along the lower part of the track which eventually climbs over Bwlch y Rhiwgyr. So far along this turn south-west on a grassy track to Sylfaen Farm and Llwyn-onn and so down the lane to Barmouth.

A gentler, low level route that gives a good flavour of the secret, wooded foothills above the Mawddach goes up the Panorama Road out of Barmouth. Turn off to the right in about a mile, aiming for the famous Panorama Walk. This track is the original road from Dolgellau to Barmouth, before the new route was created along the north shore of the Mawddach. Take time to visit the actual Panorama View, just right of the track. It really is an amazing belvedere and gives broad prospects of the estuary and Cadair Idris in clear conditions.

St. Phillip's Church, Caerdeon, near Barmouth.

Looking west down the Mawddach estuary from above Caerdeon.

Continue down the track as it descends through the woods to reach Cutiau and the mouth of the Afron Dwynant. Immediately after crossing the river turn up the steep, narrow lane (left) into the secret Glan-dwr valley. Beyond the former Goetre Mill keep right to reach the former Moriah Chapel (holiday home) and turn down right where dense conifers now block the little valley with their sombre hues. The lane swings right round, crosses a miniature pass beyond a lovely old house and drops eventually to join the main road. We, though, take a little path that forks left not far beyond the house, just where the lane begins its fall to the main road.

The path curves down across a step, lush and woody hillside overlooking the hamlet of Caerdeon. Here there is a beautiful and unusual church in the Spanish style and here, too, is Caerdeon House where Charles Darwin spent the summer with his family in 1869. The way continues through rhododendrons with glimpses of the estuary not far below. It soon comes down to the main road and a quarter mile walk eastwards brings us to Bontddu village. Here there is a choice of bus ride back to town or a steep pull up the lane near Bontddu Hall Hotel. At the top of this lane there are various interesting paths across the foothills to Barmouth.

> ". . . all these mountains
> Have in them heavenly music".

43

Penmaenpool Bridge, looking north in July.

Epilogue

So there it is; some thoughts and memories of the beautiful Mawddach and the busy port-cum-resort at its mouth. Few Welsh resorts have such a fine physical setting as Barmouth, the old settlement built on narrow ledges "carved out of that hill which protects the town beneath from cold eastern winds".

Then there is the famous beach that stretches north for several miles, past the mouth of the Afon Ysgethin at Tal-y-bont to the great sand dunes of Morfa Dyffryn and Mochras (Shell Island) and the mouth of the Afon Artro near Llanbedr. This beach was described in 1909 as "a fine smooth sand, and is deservedly popular among children and bathers". It was one of the major causes of Barmouth becoming such a popular early beach resort.

Seen from these sands "the appearance of the town is peculiarly romantic and is said to resemble strongly the fortification of Gibraltar". Many local residents liked this comparison and one tiny street of the old, hillside town came to be known as "Gibraltar Lane".

Looking south across the mouth of the Mawddach to Friog and Fairbourne from above Llanaber Road.

45

The author's parents, Rachel and Arthur Redfern, on board "Surprise" in the Irish Sea, June 1932.

It is the high ground backing Barmouth's golden coast and incomparable estuary, though, that retain much of the character of earlier times. The rugged heights of the Harlech Dome that was the happy hunting ground of Bill Tilman look across the Mawddach to the great northern side of Cadair Idris. The young Owen Glynne Jones (1867 - 99) came with his sister to stay at their cousin's home,"The Moorings", Porkington Terrace overlooking the harbour, and began his walking and scrambling here during these annual summer holidays. During May of 1888 he made the first ascent of Cyfrwy's East Arete on Cadair Idris, something of an innovative route for Wales. Jones, of course, became probably the best rock climber of his generation, a career cut short by his death on the West Arete of the Dent Blanche, Switzerland in August, 1899.

Barmouth evolved into a genteel resort during Victoria's reign and on into the early twentieth century. Many believe the place lost its way post 1945, attempting to attract Midlands' masses instead of following the low profile example of resorts like Criccieth. The heart of modern Barmouth is not a pretty place; loud "amusements" and candy floss do not sit happily alongside the old town or the lovely heights behind.

The topography hasn't allowed a by-pass for the busy A496 road so traffic is forced to add to the misery at holiday times. The hordes that flock into the town from the huge caravan parks that blemish the coastal lowland near Llanaber, Tal-y-bont and Dyffryn Ardudwy may keep the shops busy but do no favours for the ambience of the place.

Even so, one need only wander up the narrow lanes that climb the rocky ledges behind old Barmouth and in a matter of minutes you are away from the urban frenzy and back in the natural world which crowds so closely around the town.

Shearing time. The author and his mother at Llwyn-onn Bach.

Up here we are in country that Ruskin, Darwin, Owen Glynne Jones and Fanny Talbot would immediately recognise. And if we tread a little higher to come in view of Diffwys and far Cadair Idris beyond the Mawddach we'll be able to agree with E. Rosalie Jones, writing almost a century ago, that such prospects remind us of "... the Hand that surrounded us with the blue and purple hills and the emerald and sapphire waves that forever toss their white foam upon the yellow sands they lap."

Further Reading

- History of Barmouth and Vicinity.
  E. Rosalie Jones *(John Evans & Nephew, Barmouth, 1909).*

- Snowdonia.
  North, Campbell & Scott *(Collins New Naturalist Series, 1949).*

- Eryri, The Mountains of Longing.
  Amory Lovins *(Friends of the Earth, 1971).*

- Rambles in North Wales.
  Roger Redfern *(Sigma, 1993).*

Maps

OS Outdoor Leisure 1:25,000:
- Sheet 18 *(Harlech, Porthmadog & Bala/ Y Bala).*

- Sheet 23 *(Cadair Idris & Bala Lake/ Llyn Tegid).*